H Aylmer

Transformers and Spiritual Chameleons

H Aylmer

Transformers and Spiritual Chameleons

ISBN/EAN: 9783337424190

Printed in Europe, USA, Canada, Australia, Japan

Cover: Foto ©Andreas Hilbeck / pixelio.de

More available books at **www.hansebooks.com**

TRANSFORMERS

AND

SPIRITUAL CHAMELEONS

BY

MAJOR-GENERAL H. AYLMER.

"We wrestle not with flesh and blood, but against principalities, against powers, against the rulers of the darkness of this world, against spiritual wickedness in high places."—EPHES. vi. 10-19.

"O our God, wilt Thou not judge them? For we have no might against this great company that cometh against us; neither know we what to do; but our eyes are upon thee."—2 CHRON. xx. 12.

"These shall make war with the Lamb, and the Lamb shall overcome them: for He is Lord of lords, and King of kings: and they that are with Him, are called, and chosen, and faithful."—REV. xvii. 14.

LONDON:

JAMES NISBET & CO., 21 BERNERS STREET, W.

1891.

Prayer.

O GOD THE FATHER, I beseech Thee, give me the HOLY SPIRIT, that I may receive full benefit from all in this Book that agrees with Thy Holy Word, and that I may be kept from harm, if anything in it be erroneous, for the LORD JESUS CHRIST'S sake. Amen.

Reader! you are affectionately entreated to consider prayerfully the following passages of GOD'S Holy Scriptures, viz:—

John xiv. 6, 13, 14, 15, 16.—James i. 5, 6, 7, 17; iv. 2 to 10.—John vii. 37, 38, 39, xiv. 16, 17, 26; xvi. 7 to 14.—John vi. 63.—1 Thess. i. 5, 6, with 1 Cor. ii. 1 to 15.—Rom. viii. 26.—Eph. vi. 18.—1 Peter i. 2, 22 to 25.—1 John ii. 20, 27.—Luke xi. 9 to 12.

" From all sedition, privy conspiracy, and rebellion ; from all false doctrine, heresy, and schism; from hardness of heart, and contempt of Thy Word and Commandments, Good Lord, deliver us."

" That it may please Thee to illuminate all Bishops, Priests, and Deacons with true knowledge and understanding of Thy Word ; and that both by their preaching and living they may set it forth, and shew it accordingly; We beseech Thee to hear us, good Lord."

" That it may please Thee to bring into the way of truth all such as have erred and are deceived ; and that it may please Thee to give to all Thy people increase of grace to hear meekly Thy Word, and to receive it with pure affection, and to bring forth the fruits of the Spirit ; We beseech Thee to hear us, O Lord."

" O God, merciful Father, that despisest not the sighing of a contrite heart, nor the desire of such as be sorrowful, mercifully assist our prayers that we make before Thee in all our troubles and adversities, whensoever they oppress us ; and graciously hear us, that those evils which the craft or subtilty of the devil or man worketh against us, be brought to nought; and by the providence of Thy goodness they may be dispersed ; that we, Thy servants, being hurt by no persecutions, may evermore give thanks unto Thee in Thy Holy Church, through Jesus Christ.

O Lord, arise, help us, and deliver us for Thy Name's sake."

Litany of the Church of England.

"God hath chosen the foolish things of the world to confound the wise ; and God hath chosen the weak things of the world to confound the things which are mighty ; and base things of the world, and things which are despised, hath God chosen, and things which are not, to bring to nought things that are ; that no flesh should glory in His presence.

"But of Him are ye in Christ Jesus, who of God is made unto us wisdom, and righteousness, and sanctification, and redemption :

"That, according as it is written, he that glorieth, let him glory in the Lord" (1 Cor. i. 27-31).

ERRATA.

Introduction, page xvii.—For *lucit* read *lucet*.

Introduction, page xxiii., lines 7 and 15.—For Carns read Carus.

Introduction, page xxiv., line 12.—For constitute read contain.

Page 26, Note, line 5.—For Non-National read Non-Natural.

Page 26, Note, line 19. — For Tammur read Tammuz.

Page 43, line 17.—Read, "I did not say it," and omit the words—query *not*—in brackets.

Page 45, line 2. — The note of interrogation should be omitted.

Page 71, line 8.—Read, "and that we may believe," &c.

Page 84, line 5. — For unfortunate read unregenerate.

Page 142, line 12.—For Carns read Carus.

Page 177, line 19.—For assents read asserts.

SUMMARY.

Tʜᴇ last conflict between the Church of Rome and the Protestant Churches.—Archbishop Usher, Dr. Thomas Goodwin, and others, thereon.

The Oxford Tractarian Movement of 1833.—Its original programme, including Roman Sacerdotalism, Disestablishment of the Protestant Church of England, and a veiled conspiracy against England.—Remarkable anticipation of that Movement by Dr. Goodwin, the eminent Puritan divine, in his Exposition of Rev. xi., xiii., and xviii.

Characteristics of Dr. Newman and other leaders.—Their effects illustrated by some of their disciples, as disclosed in "The Morality of Tractarianism."—Dr. Newman's use of the science of "Economy."—Dean Goode, the Rev. Charles Kingsley, the Bishop of Ossory, and others, on Dr. Newman's teaching.

Count Cavour on "A Free Church in a Free State."—The schemes of bishops, clergy, and others, for "Home Re-union" and "The Unity of Christendom," with the ulterior results thereof in the light of history and analogy.—Canon Rawstorne's views thereon.

a *

Has the Church of Rome given to Europe and other parts of the world a higher and more beneficial morality than they have derived, under God's blessing, from Bible Protestantism, since the Reformation of the sixteenth century?

Does the Church of Rome, in her CANON LAW, her Trentine Catechism, her Confessional System, her Moral Theology, and otherwise, produce the opposite of morality, taking that phrase in its widest sense?—Dr. De Sanctis, the Rev. Hobart Seymour, M. Sauvestre, Arthur Guinness, Esq., and others, on those questions.

Bishop Jewel's unanswered challenge, engaging to join the Church of Rome, if the Roman Catholic authorized theologians and historical authors could refute his statements against their fundamental dogmas. —The System of the Church of Rome one of FEAR and DOUBT.

Is the Church of Rome the Spiritual Babylon of the Book of Revelation; and the Man of Sin, and Son of Perdition, and Mystery of Iniquity of 2 Thess. ii.? —Archbishop Usher, Hooker, Bishop Jewel, Bishop Christopher Wordsworth, and others, on these questions.

Bishop McIlvaine and Hooker on the Scripture teaching of our justification before God.

Bishop McIlvaine's beautiful state of mind, in prospect of death at any moment from heart complaint.

Thoughts on the MASS, and the Ritualistic Euchar-
istic Sacrifice based on the doctrine of what is called
" The Real Presence."—Holy Scripture's voice thereon.
—Archbishop Usher, Bishop Jewel, and others, thereon.

On " False Christs," " False Apostles," and Empty.
Shrines in Chancels, on pseudo-Altars, and elsewhere.

Parallels between Pagan Babylon and Spiritual
Babylon.

INTRODUCTION.

THE courteous reader is hereby informed that this book has not been compiled for philosophers, nor for scientific experts, nor for learned men, whether intellectually or theologically. It is intended mainly for such of the laity as, through pre-occupation, owing to a variety of causes, have not been led to a particular consideration of the subjects treated, nor to a knowledge of the books and publications either quoted or mentioned in the following pages, and which, as the writer feels sure, will, with God's blessing, be found of great service in these days of multiplying snares and increasing peril.

The writer claims neither a good style, nor an orthodox literary form. But whilst his own part may be viewed as sand, or earth, or any other receptacle, he ventures to hope that the Christian and candid reader will find embedded some valuable gems and golden nuggets deserving of thoughtful and prayerful consideration.

He refers in particular to the contributions

from Archbishop Usher, Bishop Jewel, Hooker, Bishop Christopher Wordsworth, Bishop McIlvaine, and Bishop Ryle.

A prominence has been assigned to Holy Scripture. For the writer believes it to be the only effectual panacea for the moral and social evils, the cares, woes, and sorrows of the Human Family. When applied to the heart and mind by that Holy Spirit who, in His great love and in His infinite wisdom, caused it to be written, it is still found, as for all the centuries of its existence it has shown itself, "the power of God unto salvation to every one that believeth;" the guide of our steps through life, the solace of all sorrow and every trouble, the support afforded to old age, and Christ, its life and light, our hope in death.

However valuable other books may be—and many are exceedingly so—yet the Bible alone, in a *unique* sense, is "given by inspiration of God," and "is profitable for doctrine, for reproof, for correction, for instruction in righteousness, that the man of God may be perfect, throughly furnished unto all good works."

Moreover, it will be found in a coming Day, the Final Court of Appeal, and the deciding

Rule for all the opinions, religions, and practices of men. This, notwithstanding all the assaults and injuries perpetrated against it by Infidels, Jewish priests, and Romish or Ritualistic hierarchists, all of whom make it of none effect by their traditions,"* and despite also all the perversions of Socinians, or the scepticizing efforts of clerical or other upholders of what is known as the "higher criticism," but which, as the writer thinks, is only some form or other of practical atheism.†

What our blessed Lord and Master has spoken in words that have been verified to this day, shall surely remain true for ever. "The Scripture cannot be broken."‡ "Heaven and

---

* Matt. xv. 1-9.

† On the subject of "Practical Atheism," the reader is referred to the sublime and deeply spiritual, as well as most attractive work on "The Attributes of God," by Stephen Charnock, one of the most illustrious of the great Puritan divines of the seventeenth century. Perhaps it is the greatest work on that subject in our language. Professor McCosh has written the introduction to the works of Charnock, in the Series of the Puritan Divines published by Messrs. Nichol, of Edinburgh. The Discourse on the Wisdom of God in Redemption, and especially with respect to the Incarnation of Christ, and the needed perfections of the Mediator, presents the *why* and *wherefore* of the two natures in our Redeemer, in a most beautiful and convincing manner. Various editions of the work on the attributes of God have been published, one by the Religious Tract Society, 56, Paternoster Row.

‡ John x. 35.

earth shall pass away, but My words shall not pass away."* "All flesh is as grass, and all the glory of man as the flower of grass. The grass withereth, and the flower thereof falleth away; but the word of the Lord endureth for ever."† After all the centuries that the Bible has existed, after all the assaults to which it has been subjected, and, notwithstanding all that has been said or shown respecting errors in transcribers, or of difficulties and perplexities in regard to the received text, is it not most wonderful that, including the learned labours and acute critical scrutiny of the last Revisionists, embracing scholars of various Churches and of different schools of thought, not a single fundamental doctrine necessary for our salvation and education for a holy heaven has been lost? On the other hand, ancient languages, inscriptions, and symbols deciphered in our days have more and more verified its historical statements; and the circulation of the Holy Scriptures throughout the world, in manifold languages and dialects, is still on the increase, ever bringing additional trophies to the feet of our adorable Redeemer.

---

* Mark xiii. 31 ; Matt. v. 17, 18.   † 1 Peter i. 23-25.

Vain are the oppositions of such poisonous books as "Lux Mundi," clouding the "Light of the World." Better far the Gospel doctrines of the Waldensian Church, with its symbol of a light clearly burning, and its appropriate motto, "*lux lucit in tenebris*." Alas for the deeply affecting truth, that "the light shineth in darkness, and the darkness comprehended it not"! (John i. 1-5).

Truly has our Christian poet Cowper said :—

> "Errors in the heart breed errors in the brain,
> And these reciprocally breed again."

Is not the authenticity, genuineness, and special inspiration of the Holy Bible, from its internal evidence, particularly as regards its wondrous unity, a mine comparatively unexplored and unrevealed?

How eminently suggestive, for instance, and how enlightening are such comparisons as those between :

(1.) Gen. ii. 21-23 ; Ephes. v. 23-29 ; 1 Tim. ii. 13, 14 ; John x. 11-18.

(2.) Gen. iii. 1-7, 13 ; 2 Cor. xi. 1-3, 13-15 ; Heb. ii. 14-18; John vi. 66-71 ; 2 Thess. ii. 3-12 ; 1 Tim. iv. 1-5.

Whilst learned critics seek to shake our

confidence in the authenticity of the book of
Genesis, in the reality of its account of man's
fall through the temptation of Eve by the fallen
angel Satan,* and of the importance of the first
promise of a Saviour,† whose actual fulfilment
we know ; the great Apostle Paul stops not to
prove the divinely sealed authenticity of the Fall
recorded in Gen. iii. 1-7 ; but applies it practically
with most impressive force in 2 Cor. xi. Are we
not in our own days witnessing in the history of
the Papacy the fuller developments of the
warnings and prophecies in the second group of
texts noted above ?

Or. to take one more illustration, in Gen.
iii. 2-3 compared with Gen. ii. 16, 17, the
subtlety of the temptation lies in the sophistical
misuse of the plural " trees " as opposed
to the singular " tree." " Of *every* tree,
pleasant to the eye, and good for food," our
first parents might "freely" eat, "without money
and without price." *Only one* tree was
prohibited, not simply as a *minimum test*
of their love, loyalty, and obedience, but

* Luke x. 18-20 ; Jude 6 ; John viii. 44 ; 1 Tim. iii. 6 ; 2 Cor.
xi. 13-15 ; John xiv. 30 ; Matt. iv. 1-11 ; Heb. ii. 14-16 ; Col.
ii. 13-15 ; Rev. xii. 7-12, 17.

† Gen. iii. 13-15 : Gal. iii. 16.

also, as they were graciously and kindly warned, because disobedience would entail on our first parents grievous harm. Our heavenly Father might have given to His creatures a simple prohibitory command. But as "God is Love," He not only interposed a merciful injunction between them and the deadly tree, but, additionally, warned them with lovingkindness against it. The Tempter came not as "an open enemy" to "do dishonour" to God, and to injure the happy pair. He came not as an infidel, but allowed the existence of the Creator against whom he had sinned. Mixing up truth and falsehood, he put a scepticizing question, susceptible of two opposite interpretations: "Yea, hath God said, Ye shall *not* eat of *every* tree of the garden ?" (Gen. iii. 1). In one sense of God's Word, He had not said so. In another sense, infused by a subtly-used misinterpretation, it was so far true, that *one* tree that was injurious was excluded. Thus, Satan sought to infuse a "fiery dart" of doubt as to the perfect and immutable love and goodness of God.

Are we not living in days when the very same devices are in operation, after some six

thousand years, by the same ceaseless foe ? Are
we not perplexed and all the more imperilled
by strange mixtures of a certain amount of Bible
truth in combination with soul-destroying error ?
Does not the voice from the *pulpit,* in some of
our churches and chapels, *seem* to preach a
Gospel sermon, whilst from the chancel, and
before *an altar-wise structure, or a pseudo-altar* of
a Romish type, " a different gospel,"* is preached
objectively and otherwise, in other words, rank
Popery ? The enhanced peril to souls from that
course of procedure by the Church of Rome is
powerfully shown by HOOKER in the extracts
given from his golden discourse on Justification.
Also from another standpoint by Bishop Christopher Wordsworth, as will be seen.   Other
eminent witnesses to the same effect could not
be quoted in the limited space available to the
writer.

Sceptics, who treat the Bible account of the
Fall of man as a mere allegory, necessarily deny
the need of our Redemption through Christ.
They destroy Christianity, and have no hope of
happiness beyond the grave, based on a revelation from God.

* Gal. i. 6-7, R.V.

On the other hand, the Church of Rome's doctrine of the immaculate conception of the Virgin Mary, although the Bible declares that, since the Fall, "there is none righteous, no not one" (Rom. iii. 9-11, 20), and although that holy and lovely character, the Virgin Mary, trusted not to her own righteousness, but "rejoiced in God her Saviour" (Luke i. 46, 47)—that doctrine of the Church of Rome involves, of necessity, the assertion that her parents also were sinless, and so on upwards to our first parents. Thus, equally with infidels, Rome, in effect, denying the Fall and its consequences to all mankind, overturns the foundation of Christianity.

What is our best arm? It is set forth in Ephes. vi., "The sword of the Spirit, which is the Word of God," the "two-edged sword" figuratively proceeding from Christ's mouth,* with its Old Testament edge and its New Testament edge forming the one irresistible *Instrument* when used by the Holy Spirit as the *Agent*, that is the weapon to be used in faith, which faith is God's free gift to all who, through grace, will, from the heart, ask for

---

Rev i. 16, ii. 12, 16; xix. 15, 21.

it perseveringly in the name of Christ, our great High Priest and Intercessor.

As long as Eve kept to the Word of God, she was safe, and the Tempter could not overcome her. How beautiful is her clear discrimination, in her perfect state, between what appertained in God's Word to " the *trees*," and what alone to " the *tree*"! (Gen. iii. 2, 3), and though neither she nor her husband could comprehend in their unfallen state what was meant by *death*, whether spiritual or physical, yet, that their unclouded faculties understood that it was *something harmful* is clear from Eve's addition of two most noteworthy words, namely, the words " *touch not*, lest ye die."

Do not the foregoing considerations help to light up with suggestive force the love and mercy of Christ when He warningly says, "Whosoever therefore shall be ashamed of Me and of My words in this adulterous and sinful generation, of him also shall the Son of Man be ashamed when He cometh in the glory of His Father with the holy angels " ? *

As Romish and Ritualistic enemies of the REFORMATION of the sixteenth century, and of

---

* Mark viii. 38.

BIBLE PROTESTANTISM, are still found charging " Protestantism," as they vaguely term it, with being merely negative and " destructive," but not " constructive," some effort has been made by the writer to obviate that untenable representation, not only from the writings of Hooker, but also by adding from Canon Carns' widely known and precious " Memorials of Bishop McIlvaine," the beautiful and peaceful sentiments of that holy and eminent American Bishop, in the prospect of death at any moment, from heart complaint. They afford a striking illustration of the efficacy of those Gospel doctrines, which the Bishop embodied in what Canon Carns terms—and which thousands of Christ's servants will endorse—that learned prelate's " great work " on " *Righteousness by Faith.*"

Oh, that even a majority of our present bishops were like-minded with him ! Oh, that " by their preaching and living " they set forth a full Gospel, and made it evident by eschewing themselves, and setting their faces faithfully against clergymen introducing human tradi- tions, that they are really " persuaded," accord- ing to their declaration before the Archbishop, "that the Holy Scriptures contain sufficiently all doctrine required of necessity for eternal salvation through faith in Jesus Christ"! Oh, that whilst consistently setting the example themselves, they would only countenance and honour such clergymen in their dioceses as show themselves thoroughly true to their solemn Ordination vows, "with all faithful diligence, to banish and drive away all erroneous and strange doctrines contrary to God's Word," especially such as are embodied in the Thirty-nine Articles, *which constitute the true doctrine of the Church of England,*" in particular against the fundamental doctrines and practices of the Church of Rome ! Alas, that an opposite course should be so strangely and so glaringly mani-fested ! What are the laity to think of the external pomp, the theatrical Eucharistic vest-ments, the Popish mitres, and other bedizen-ments affected by some of our bishops, painfully reminding us of those characteristics of the Church of Rome prophesied of in Rev. xviii. ?

Is it not very sad that the laity are helpless under such a state of things, and that an in-creasing number, whether of those who seek, through grace, to be faithful to Christ and His

Gospel truth, or of others who dislike clerical glare and glitter, priestly assumptions, sensuous worship, proxy musical services, intoning and multiplied pu stures, are driven from their parish churches ?

Bishop Wordsworth, with reference to Rev. xvii. 1-6, in his book on " Union with Rome," points out that, in Scripture, " a faithless Church may be called an *Adulteress* because she forsakes God, but she may also be, and often is, called in Scripture, a *Harlot*, when she mixes false doctrine and worship with the true faith.

"The original word," he adds, "which is uniformly used for *harlot*, by St. John in the Apocalypse, is πόρνη (*porné*). It, ' or its derivatives,' is used at least *fifty times* to describe the spiritual fornication, that is, the *corrupt doctrine* and *practice* of the Churches of Israel and Judah ; and so *Samaria* herself, or the Church of Israel, which Bossuet specifies as the proper parallel, is charged with *harlotry*.

" Therefore, the word *harlot* does designate a *church*, and if the Church of Rome is described by that name in the Apocalypse, then the word *harlot*, as applied to her, indicates *the multitude of her sins* " (pp. 37, 38. Italics in original).

b *

Now, the Divine command respecting spiritual Babylon, or the Church of Rome, is, *Come out of her!* (Rev. xiii. 11-18, xiv. 6-11, xvii. 1-6, xviii.). What, then, are we to think of the conduct of the Archbishop of Canterbury and his prelatic assessors in their recent judgment? They have not only over-ridden the contrary decisions of the highest legal court in England, on the points charged against the Bishop of Lincoln ; but, besides dismissing the majority of those charges, they have, so far as lay in their power, legalized Bishop King's glaring Romanizing doctrines and practices,* and, in so doing, have defied the Divine injunction, and have said, in effect, to our bishops, clergy, and laity, *" Go into her "* !

Again, in Rev. xiv. 9, a most solemn prohibition is found against "receiving the mark" of "Babylon," which the Church of England, in her Homilies, proclaims to be the Church of Rome. To "receive the mark, number, and name" signifies that men *"devote themselves to the Papal Antichrist"* (Elliott, " Horæ Apocalypticæ," 3rd ed., vol. iii., p. 218).

A fearful woe is denounced against such as receive the " mark." It is said that " the same

---

* See the remarks from the *Times* of November 25th, in the Appendix. Also, the enlightening views of Lord Halifax, President of the English Church Union, on the Judgment, and on " The Continuity of the Church of England."

shall drink of the wine of the wrath of God"
(Rev. xiv. 10), and because of "partaking of
[Babylon's] sins, they shall receive of her plagues"
(Rev. xviii. 4-8).

Have we not alarming cause, then, to appre-
hend righteous retributive judgments on our
National Church and our Nation from the apos-
tatizing doings of our bishops and clergy, and
their abettors ?

Do not the awakening illustrations of Bishop
Wordsworth remind us vividly of the national
judgments, including repeated invasions of their
land, and their eventual banishment and disper-
sion to this day of the kingdoms of Judah and
Israel on account of the wicked backslidings,
idolatries, and iniquities of their priesthood and
people ?

Is it not written, "Unto whomsoever much
is given, of him shall much be required" ? (Luke
xii. 48). Has not England received higher
benefits, religious and political, than even God's
ancient people enjoyed ? Have we not deep
cause, then, to tremble at the judicial and correc-
tive rebukes and chastenings that we may expect to suffer if our rulers in Church and State
sin against God worse than did Judah and

b 2 *

Israel? Do not the words of the prophet apply to us, "A wonderful and horrible thing is committed in the land. The prophets prophesy falsely, and the priests bear rule by their means, and my people love to have it so: and what will ye do in the end thereof"? (Jer. v. 30, 31).

What is before us? Archbishop USHER, in his latter years, was of decided opinion that the last great battle between Rome and the Protestant Churches, and the final persecution unto death of Protestant witnesses, was still future. His views were expressed in a Life of the Archbishop by his Chaplain, Dr. Bernard. They will be found in the form of an Appendix to the old edition of that remarkable work on prophecy by the Rev. Robert Fleming, entitled, "Apocalyptic Key: An Extraordinary Discourse on the Rise and Fall of Papacy" (London, 1793).

"The Archbishop," says his Chaplain, Dr. Bernard, "foretold the *Irish rebellion* forty years before it came to pass, with the very time when it should break forth, in a sermon preached in Dublin in 1601, where, from Ezek. iv. 6, *discoursing concerning the prophets bearing the iniquity of Judah forty days, the Lord therein appointed a day for a year; he made this direct application in relation to the Government's connivance at Popery to that time.* From *this year* (says he) will I reckon the sin of *Ireland,* that those *whom you now embrace* shall be your ruin, and *you* shall bear this iniquity. Which prediction proved exactly true; for from that time, 1601, to the year 1641, was just forty years, in which it is notoriously known that the *rebellion* and *destruction of Ireland happened,* which was accomplished by those Popish priests and other Papists, who were then connived at and encouraged. . . . . Lastly," adds Dr. Bernard, "the Archbishop foretold that ' the *greatest stroke upon the Reformed Churches was yet to come,* and that the time of the utter ruin of the See of *Rome should be when she thought herself most secure,'** and as to this last, I shall add a brief account from the person's own hand,

---

* In connection with Usher's views, see Rev. xi. 7 ; xviii. 5-8.

The Church of Rome now regards herself as a *Widow,* having lost her husband *the State,* or the *Temporal Power.* Before the Vatican Council met, M. Louis Veuillot, the editor of the leading Ultramontane journal in France, *L'Univers,* remarked, with surprise, that not a single Roman Catholic crowned head had, according to the precedent of centuries, been invited to the Council. It is an anachronism in history, he said. What does it mean ? *What else but a divorce between the Church and the State is thereby proclaimed ?*

In that view, the " *Woman* " of Rev. xvii. 1-5 no longer holds the reins, and compels the State to be her executioner. She has been *unhorsed* in Rome itself. But, apparently, either actually or *virtually,*

who was concerned therein, which follows in these words.

Only some extracts from that remarkable account can here be given.

"The year before this learned and holy primate Archbishop *Usher* died,"* says the narrator, "I presumed to inquire of him what his present apprehensions were concerning a very *great persecution* which should fall upon the Church of God in these nations of *England, Scotland,* of which this reverend primate had spoken with great confidence many years before, when we were in the highest and fullest state of outward peace and settlement. I also asked him, 'Whether he did believe those sad times to be past, or that they were yet to come?' To which he answered, 'That they were yet to come, and that he did as confidently expect it as ever he had done?' Adding, 'That this sad persecution would fall upon *all the Protestant Churches in Europe.*'"

---

the Church of Rome will be able, exultingly and confidently, to "say in her heart, I sit a queen, and am *no widow,* and shall see no sorrow." (Rev. xviii. 6-7). Christ's faithful witnesses may be slain or silenced. But then will "her plagues come in one day, death, and mourning, and famine'" (vers. 8, 21).

* The Archbishop died March 21, 1655.

The narrator having stated some objections, to that dark prospect, the Archbishop said, " Fool not yourself with such hopes, for I tell you, all you have yet seen hath been but the beginning of sorrows, to what is yet *to come upon the Protestant Churches of Christ*, who will *ere long fall under a sharper persecution than ever yet was upon them:* and therefore (said he to me), *look you be not found in the outward court, but a worshipper in the temple before the altar; for Christ will measure all those that profess His name, and call themselves His people*, and the outward worshippers He *will leave out* to be *trodden down* by the Gentiles. The *outward court* (says he) is the *formal Christian*, whose religion lies in performing the outward duties of Christianity, without having *an inward life and power of faith and love uniting them to Christ;* and these God will leave to be trodden down and swept away by the Gentiles ; but the worshippers *within the temple*, and *before the altar*, are those who do *indeed* worship God *in spirit and in truth*, whose *souls* are made His temple, and He is honoured and adored in the *most inward thoughts* of their hearts, and they sacrifice their lusts and vile affections, yea, and their *own wills* to him; and *these* God will hide in the *hollow of His hand,* and *under the shadow of His wings.* . . . . As it shall be the *sharpest,* so it shall be the *shortest persecution of them all;* and shall only take away the *gross hypocrites* and *formal professors,* but the true spiritual believers shall be preserved till the calamity be over.

"He then added that the Papists were, in his opinion, the Gentiles spoken of in the xi. of the *Revelations,* to whom the *outward court should be left,* that they might tread it under foot, they having received the Gentiles' worship, in their adoring images, and saints departed, and in taking to themselves many mediators, and this (said he) the Papists are now designing among themselves, and therefore be sure you be ready "* (pp. 5, 6, 8, 10, 11, 12, 13, 14. Italics in the original).

---

* Dr. Goodwin, in his Exposition of the chapters specified, and more especially Rev. xiii, anticipated with astonishing accuracy the rise and the characteristics of Tractarianism or Ritualism. He remarked that it would appear in a Protestant church, that the party would only develop by degrees its Romish character and aims, and that they were to be the Pope's "chief janizaries" in the latter years of the Papacy. His remarkable delineation has been republished at various intervals since the Oxford Movement of 1833. Parts of his Exposition will be found in Dr. Gill's Commentary on the chapters in question.

Dr. Thomas Goodwin, one of the greatest of the illustrious Puritan divines of the seventeenth century, and a writer as modest, as free from dogmatism, and as candid in noticing objections as he was learned, has expressed convictions agreeing with those of Archbishop Usher. They will be found in his expositions of Rev. xi. 1-7, xiii. 11-18, and xviii. 1-8.

He thinks that after the Church of Rome has recovered her power over the European nations for a short time, she may at first, out of policy, and in the endeavour to remove from herself any further application of the characteristics set forth in Rev. xvii. 6, rest content for a while with closing Protestant places of worship and silencing the Protestant witnesses, but he fears that she will proceed yet further, and will persecute even unto death. The chief scene of these sufferings he thinks will be ENGLAND, where, as he observes, it may be expected that the greater number of Protestants in Europe will be found at the coming crisis and final conflict.

Bishop Christopher Wordsworth, in his booklet on "Union with Rome," expresses his conviction, based on Holy Scripture, that, if

Rome regains her power, she will persecute "with more-fury than ever."

To quote no other authors, the Presbyterian minister, the Rev. Alexander Hislop, in his work of vast research, entitled "The Two Babylons," comes to a like conclusion, from a different standpoint, namely, that, *to complete the parallel between Pagan Babylon and Spiritual Babylon*, a closing and deadly struggle for permanent supremacy must be expected on the part of the Church of Rome.

See also the late Rev. Edward Bickersteth's book, "The Divine Warning to the Church."

It remains for the writer to express his best thanks to a very able friend, whose writings are highly valued in the Protestant Churches, not only in this country, but also in our colonies, and further still, for his important advice, and for his kind examination of the "Thoughts on the Romish Mass and the Ritualistic Eucharistic Sacrifice" at the end of this book. The matter on those points, and the inferences drawn from the Church of Rome's Catechism, have his concurrence. From that friend's thorough knowledge of the controversy with Rome, his opinion has greatly encouraged the writer, who would gladly, if allowed, divulge his name.

Some prayers have been added, in the earnest hope that brethren of the Church of England may be induced to unite in using them; and that Christian brethren in other Churches may, at any rate, as they may prefer, lift up their hearts to the throne of grace, on behalf of the objects suggested.

In addition to the testimony with respect to the Church of Rome's Confessional System, the pernicious nature of the official treatises studied by her priesthood, and her "*transformation*" of Bible Christianity, the following remarks of Dr. Desanctis* deserve careful consideration :—

Rome was his native place. For fourteen years he exercised the office of confessor, and for seven years he held the post of parish priest in Rome. He was Professor of Theology, and official Theological Censor of the Inquisition, &c., and thus, "in conformity with Papal usage, was brought into intimate relations with the secret police, and," adds Mr. Buckle, "would be

---

* The above sketch is compiled briefly from Dr. Desanctis' book entitled, "Confession: A Doctrinal and Historical Essay," translated from the 18th Italian edition by H. M. G. Buckle, Vicar of Ellingham (S. W. Partridge, 1878), and from "The Jesuits: An Historical Sketch," by E. W. Grinfield, M.A. (Seeley, 1853), Note 20. The first part of Dr. Desanctis' work was published by The Religious Tract Society.

introduced behind the scenes of the religious and political drama enacted at the Papal See."

Pius IX. entertained a great esteem for Dr. Desanctis. He was "appointed to deliver a course of lectures against heretics, and received a licence to read their works." * In the over-ruling providence of God, "gradually the light of Divine truth dawned more and more clearly on his mind." He left the Church of Rome, and became a minister of the Reformed Italian Church at Geneva.

"Rome," say Dr. Desanctis, "is the city which surpasses all the other cities of Italy in immorality. But perhaps the blame ought to be imputed to the Roman people? No; the Roman people, noble, generous as their fore-fathers, would be the people of the greatest virtue, an heroic people, if it were trained to virtue, if it were educated in the Gospel. But all the fine qualities of that people are stifled by the teaching of its Church, and the people is brutalized in guilt. *Blasphemy against God is the predominant vice of the Roman ;*† but the

---

* Buckle, Preface ix, x.

† Is not the above terrible feature a startling illustration of the wonderful prophetic anticipations of the inspired book of Revelation. The subjects of the Apostate Church were to be "full of the names of

blasphemer confesses, departs absolved, and is
no sooner out of the Church than he begins to
blaspheme anew. Drunkenness, murder, theft,
fraud, adultery, are crimes incessantly repeated,
but whoever commits them confesses, and
believes himself absolved; and immorality is not
only not assisted, but by the facility of pardon
at the cost of a few prayers is committed again
without scruple."

Up to 1848, at least, there were " not fifty
persons in so vast a city who did not confess."
" Yet, with so many confessions, immorality
was ever on the increase, and vice was triumphant, and the increase was greatest (I speak
of notorious facts) in those who were most
regular in confession ; and to them is Rome
indebted for the current proverb, ' Better an
unbeliever than a bigot.' " *

In allusion to the SYSTEM of the Church of
Rome, Dr. Desanctis says, " Despotism and
tyranny are loudly condemned by the Gospel ;

---

blasphemy" (Rev. xvii. 3). How could the blasphemies [or, *the
dishonouring of God*] in the Mass, in Mariolatry, in creature worship,
in other forms, in many mediators, &c., &c., fail to produce correspond-
ing fruits in a people so indoctrinated ?

The italics not in the original. ‡

* Pp. 108, 109.

but the Popes, in order to be despots and tyrants,
and to raise crowned pupils for their school,
have substituted their decrees for the Gospel.
. . . . Infidels, profiting by such a disposi-
tion of the nations, have disseminated their
irreligious principles, and to the Popes must be
attributed the irreligion of the nations.

"Nor can it be alleged that certain Popes have
misused religion, and that the abuses ought
therefore to be attributed to the individual, and
not to the system. From Sylvester to our
time, all the Popes, some more, some less, *have
contributed to* TRANSFORM* *the religion of Jesus
Christ*, and to build up the system of oppression
and political annihilation on the ruins of liberty
and progress. Nay, the very Popes who have
been most conspicuous in this work of destruction are adored as heroes on the altars of Rome."†

Dr. Desanctis entirely confirms the state-

---

*Amongst transformers and transformations the JESUITS, perhaps,
have obtained the pre-eminence. One week dressed as a British work-
man, and introducing discord, strife, and lawlessness, the same Jesuit
may, next week, hold some important position in a Court, or on the
staff of a Prime Minister in some other part of Europe, or may be engaged in some other capacity. So, also, female Jesuits may be occu-
pied as governesses in families, or as lady superiors in sisterhoods, or
in various positions of society. They may do the work of the Jesuits
without belonging to any particular order.

† Pp. 145, 146.

ments adduced by Mr. Hobart Seymour and others quoted in this volume on the frightful evils of the confessional.

" How, he asks, " can it happen otherwise, if immorality, thanks to confession, is reduced by Catholic priests to scientific principles ? The most shameful libertine could not read without blushing the filth which is contained in the books of moral theology ; and it is upon these books that the education of the young clergy in the seminaries is formed."*

No wonder that Dr. Desanctis' book " com- municated a shock to the Papacy in Italy, under which," says Mr. Buckle, " it continues to reel and stagger to this hour."†

In addition to other important works men- tioned in the following pages, the writer has derived much help from the "Horæ Apocalyticæ " (5th ed.), by the Rev. E. B. Elliott ; " " The Approaching End of the Age," and " The Divine Drama of the World's History," by Dr. Grattan Guinness; and the Exposition of the Apocalypse on the basis of Bengel and Elliott, in the "Critical New Testament;" and he is sure that further valuable aid will be found in the Manuals

---

* Pp. 111, 112.   † Preface, p. vii.

on the Romish Controversy by the Rev. Charles
Stanford, M.A., and by the Rev. Dr. Blakeney ;
also in a carefully compiled historical pamphlet
by the Rev. Thomas Waller, A.B., entitled,
"Laudism, or the Agreement between the
British and Foreign Protestant Churches in
Reformation Times" (Dublin : George Herbert).
The three volumes of tracts published by the
Church Association are a treasury of information
and an armoury on Ritualism. (See also their
"Churchwarden's Guide.")

Now, for whatever is Scriptural, wise, or good
in this book, all honour and all praise be to Him
who is the Father of lights, from whom "every
good gift and every perfect gift cometh down"
(James i. 17). May CHRIST, who is the "LIGHT
OF THE WORLD" (John viii. 12), the Life, the
Light and the Key to the Holy Bible, and the
Centre of all History, be alone exalted !

TRANSFORMERS AND SPIRITUAL CHAMELEONS.

THE war between SCRIPTURAL, and *not merely political*, PROTESTANTISM on the one hand, and ROMANISM and RITUALISM on the other hand, is becoming more intensified from day to day.

It may be that the last culminating battle, anticipated by eminent students of prophecy, including Archbishop USHER, is not far off.

Amongst other movements having vast ulterior bearings, are those denominated "*Home Reunion*," and the "*The Unity of Christendom*," as it is called, by the Society zealously engaged in furthering its realization. Both of those movements are intimately connected with a fundamental object with certain Anglican Romanizers of the Oxford "Movement," now merged in the "Ritualists," which they express by the phrase—"The Continuity of the CHURCH,". which was broken off by the REFORMATION of the sixteenth century.

B

Ritualistic clergymen are found more or less accurately re-echoing the favourite though utterly fallacious charge brought against true Protestantism by the Tractarian leaders, that it is "*a system of negatives—destructive, not constructive,*" and, in effect, is *powerless as a moral force.*

On the other hand, the Church of Rome is held forth as the only safe and desirable CENTRE OF UNITY, and as *the* effectual Moral Force for the healing of *Society* throughout Europe and the whole world.

Thus, Dean Close, in a paper read at the annual meeting of the Evangelical Union for the Diocese of Carlisle, in 1866,* and printed and published at its request, quotes, in confirmation of the above stricture on Protestantism [from a work edited by the Rev. Orby Shipley, entitled " The Church and the World." It is a composite volume, singularly reminding us of that *mixture* of " persons of the most opposite sentiments," marking the original Oxford " Movement," a mixture well fitted to

---

* Its title is, " The Catholic Revival—or Ritualism and Romanism in the Church of England." (Hatchard & Co.) The italics and capitals are in the original.

perplex the Christian public, to allay their fears, and to promote the tactics in behalf of the sinister objects of the " Movement."

" Six or seven of these papers," says the Dean, " would do credit to any volume."

Some of the articles, he says, " are worthy of all commendation, exhibiting in a compressed form powerful arguments in favour of God's truth." But, he adds, " One keynote, one tone, one unison, one colour, one object, transparently evident, distinctly marks all the other papers, the EXPOSITION, DEFENCE, AND PROMOTION OF THE DOCTRINES AND PRACTICES OF EXTREME RITUALISM." [Sic.]

He shows how " the authors deplore the practical change which has turned OUR CLERGY from a SACRIFICING PRIESTHOOD into a PREACHING MINISTRY " (p. 236). " RITUALISM," he observes, " would turn them back again from a PREACHING MINISTRY—their Reformation character—into a SACRIFICING PRIESTHOOD, their old ROMAN CATHOLIC CHARACTER, and here lie the pith and marrow of the whole question."

" RITUALISM," he truly says, " has intimate affiance with ROMANISM, but it abjures :—

" Protestantism as hopelessly undogmatic—a

system of negatives—destructive, not constructive ; it subverts the Catholic doctrine of ' communion with Christ through the Church,'
'making an *intellectual process called* FAITH, and
a *mental conviction called apprehension of Christ
by faith*, to be the means—not the condition, but
the means—of effecting the union with Christ '"
(pp. 100, 184). [Italics and capitals in original.]

As a humble, and in various respects, most
imperfect contribution towards a right solution
of some of the foregoing questions, the following
compilation is offered for prayerful and candid
consideration :—

MORALITY will be treated in its wider meaning, as including not only unchastity, but all
sins against the Decalogue, the Sermon on the
Mount, and other Divine injunctions, as interpreted, for instance, by the inspired Apostle
Paul, who includes " the lawless and disobedient," " perjured persons," " the fearful and
unbelieving, the abominable, and murderers,
and whoremongers, and sorcerers, and idolaters,
and all liars " (1 Tim. i. 5-11 ; Rom. xiii. 8-10 ;
Matt. v. 17-19 ; Ephes. vi. 2, 3 ; Rev. xxi.
7, 8).

Whatever may be the questions discussed,

and to whichever party we may be led to adhere—after honest and persevering prayer for the Holy Spirit's teaching, in the name of Christ our alone High Priest and Intercessor—should we not, one and all of us, ever remember that "every one of us shall give account of himself to God" (Rom. xiv. 9-13), and that, therefore, as we cannot avoid our personal accountability to Christ, we cannot divest ourselves not simply of the *right* of private judgment, but of its correlative *necessity?* Consequently, must it not follow that we are bound both by Holy Scripture and by reason, to accord to others full civil and religious liberties, provided only that liberty claimed and exercised be not abused to the injury of the lives, characters, lawful privileges, and property of " our neighbour " ?

Should we not as carefully as possible distinguish between SYSTEMS and *their followers,* and righteously abstain from thinking of the *led* as we are constrained to regard their *leaders?* Are there not *moderate* High Churchmen who sincerely protest against Ritualistic Romanizers, their doctrines and their practices? Are there not varying

measures of faith, courage, and faithfulness
amongst Evangelicals and other Churchmen?
Of course, TRUTH and LOVE must never be
divorced. We must not sacrifice Truth for the
sake of *human love*, nor love *any* creature
more than CHRIST (Matt. x. 24-39; Rom.
i. 16-28).

We need not question the perfect sincerity
and conscientiousness of any man in all that he
teaches and does. But we may be sincerely and
conscientiously *wrong* as well as *right*. Our
Lord and Master warned His disciples that their
persecutors and murderers would "think that
they did God service," because they "knew not
the Father, nor Him" (John xvi. 1-4). So
acted the Apostle Paul before his conversion.
He "verily thought with himself that he OUGHT
to do many things contrary to the name of
Jesus of Nazareth." He "shut up many saints
in prison, having received authority from the
chief priests," just as the blood-thirsty Church
of Rome has used her State lay "Churchmen" (Rev. xvii. 3-6, 9, 12, 13, 15, 18) as
executioners of her will and sentences, ready
from her education of them to torture and to
slay, or fearing her terrible excommunication

if they demurred. When Christ's martyrs, Stephen and others, "were put to death, he gave his voice against them" (Acts vii. 58-60; xxii. 19, 20; xxvi. 8-15). Afterwards, he bitterly mourned that he had been "a blasphemer, and a persecutor, and injurious" (1 Tim. i. 12-14). Some of Christ's disciples wanted, in His service, to burn up certain Samaritans. "But He turned and rebuked them" (Luke ix. 54, 55). Even the holy and loving Apostle John at one time offended against Christ by intolerance. He and others "forbade" one who was serving our Lord and honouring Him, *because*, said John, "he followeth not us." *He is not in the* APOSTOLICAL SUCCESSION. "But Jesus said, Forbid him NOT" (Mark ix. 33-40).

That plain, emphatic, and far-reaching command of Christ has been systematically ignored and disobeyed by Churches and by Governments for upwards of a thousand years. Episcopalians, Presbyterians, Independents, and other Denominations have acted, more or less, in that anti-Christian spirit. PROTESTANTS who so act, do so *in direct contradiction to* their own fundamental principle, that, the HOLY BIBLE is

the alone Divine and Supreme Rule of Faith
and Practice, and final Court of Appeal. On
the other hand, ROMAN CATHOLICS so act *in
entire accordance with* their supreme rule,
which is not the written Word of God, but *its
very opposite*, as embodied in the Canons of the
Council of Trent, the Catechism of the Council
of Trent, and their fearfully intolerant, persecuting, and pitiless CANON LAW, the provisions
of which are probably unknown to the great
majority of the Church of Rome's laity, no less
than to the majority of the Protestant laity—if,
indeed—we must not add—that the terrible
character of that Canon Law is not known by
the larger proportion of the Clergy and
Ministers of our Protestant Churches. No
wonder at their fatal apathy to the spread of
Romanism and Ritualism.

Every bishop, priest, and layman is bound
to carry out that law in every Protestant
country. The dogma of INFALLIBILITY adopted
at the Vatican Council *is necessarily retrospec-
tive, and irrevocably binds every Pope and his
hierarchy to enact, wherever possible*, the san-
guinary Bulls of former Popes, with the persecuting edicts of the Councils of Lateran and

Constance, and other contents of that Canon Law.*

"History repeats itself," and "like causes produce like effects." At present, the Church of Rome has lost her temporal power. She may regain it, and at the rate things are progressing thitherwards in England and her Colonies, she probably *will* regain it for a time, if not *directly*, yet *indirectly*. Very subtle and powerful influences are at work on the part of the Pope's body guard, the Jesuits, with their conscious agents, and their unconscious catspaws in the House of Commons, and in all the Protestant Churches. The words "liberty," "religious equality" "justice," "charity,"

---

* In confirmation of the statements above, see amongst other works appealing to undeniable Roman Catholic Authority—

1. "The Nullity of the Government of Queen Victoria in Ireland," by the Rev. Robert J. McGhee, A.M. (London : Seeley & Burnside, 1841.)

2. "The Church of Rome : Her Present Moral Theology, Scriptural Instruction, and Canon Law—A Report on 'The Books and Documents of the Papacy,'" by the same author. (Partridge & Oakey, 1852.)

3. "Which Sovereign—Queen Victoria or the Pope?" by Rev. J. L. Wylie, LL.D. (London : Morgan & Scott.)

4. "The Papacy of Modern Times." (Glasgow: The Scottish Protestant Alliance.)

See also the important facts in the "Monthly Letter" of the Protestant Alliance for June, 1886, and for September and November, 1889.

"bigotry," "intolerance," *wholly inapplicable as they are in the use made of them to the wholly* UNIQUE *and altogether* EXCEPTIONAL principles and demands of the *unchangeable* Church of Rome,* are played off with marvellous success on generous, confiding, but duped, JOHN BULL. Protestant England once conquered for the Pope, then, as Cardinal Manning has truly said, "Protestantism is conquered throughout the world. Once overthrown here, all is but a war of detail." Then, as of yore, what may not be carried out by that "*semper eadem*" spiritual despotism, now earnestly striving, for her own purposes, to win over the democracy and utilize them?

That phrase, "*the continuity of the history of the* CHURCH," deserves very careful consideration, especially in connection with the Oxford "Movement," and with what one of its most influential leaders so accurately called their

---

| * That eminent Italian statesman, Count Cavour, had ample historical and other warrant for his famous aphorism, "A FREE CHURCH in A FREE STATE." But her unalterable maxim is, "A SUPREME CHURCH in AN ENSLAVED STATE." The figurative "Woman" ever wants to *hold the reins* of the typical imperial "scarlet-coloured beast" (Rev. xvii. 1-6), as the imperious murderess JEZEBEL used Ahab's State seal, and her successor "calleth herself a prophetess" (Rev. ii. 20-22).

"*poisoning*" system and their "*conspiracy.*"
The Church of England, originally independent
of the Church of Rome, was delivered from malig-
nant continuity with her by the happy events of
the Reformation.

The leader alluded to was the Rev. R. Hurrell
Froude. (See his " Remains," vol. i., pp. 317,
326, 329, 337, 390, 430.) They were edited
by the Rev. J. H. (afterwards Cardinal) Newman and the Rev. John Keble, both of whom
endorsed his opinions.*

Unhappily, bishops and clergyman in our
Protestant Church, despite their ordination
vows, are labouring to restore that continuity. In
the Army, or the Navy, in time of war, if officers
parleyed with the enemy, adopted their uni-
forms, furthered their plan of campaign, helped
to introduce them into our barracks and citadels,
and otherwise played us false, our loyal military

---

* Other leaders, or writers of books, or of tracts, were—Dr. Pusey,
Revs. W. Ward, Isaac Williams, Arthur Percival, William Palmer, Mr.
Gladstone, and others. According to "a leading Tractarian periodical,"
says Mr. Bricknell, the last three gentlemen—and, says its Editor,
" even Mr. Gladstone "—showed " an obvious wish to separate themselves in the public eye from their brethren, upon whom the storm of
popular nicknames and insults have been poured." (Bricknell's
" Judgment of the Bishops," p. 124, and " The Ritualists, or Non-
Natural Catholics," by Rev. Peter Maurice, D.D. Preface, pp. ii. iii.)

and naval authorities would act very differently to too many of our bishops.

In a copy of the original prospectus by the leaders of the Oxford " Movement" of 1833, sent to the Rev. Charles Girdlestone, Rector of Kingswinford, Staffordshire, which prospectus, as he says, "may be seen in Percival's Collection of Papers," the Tractarian Party somewhat indistinctly avowed " their affection towards *that spiritual community to which,*" as they said, " they *owed their hopes of the world to come.*" In due time, the *Church of Rome* was gradually exalted to that position. Amongst their objects was the securing of what their leaders called, with perplexing vagueness, " primitive practice in religious offices," and " the Apostolical prerogatives, order, and commission of bishops, priests, and deacons." Mr. Girdlestone, basing his remarks also on a significant letter sent to him by one of the Tractarians, together with the prospectus, points out how they *" insisted on resistance"* (precisely as Ritualistic bishops and clergy are now, with increasing lawlessness, doing) to whatever " might be apt to trench upon the high sacramental doctrines, or the high sacerdotal claims assumed to be primitive and apostolical."

"On this footing," adds Mr. Girdlestone, "the tracts, by gradual development, raised the coherent structure of ascetism, celibacy, factitious piety, and irresponsible Church authority, all of which, though neither primitive nor apostolic, had been imported from Oriental heathenism into the Church of the first three centuries," preparing the way for "Mediæval Popery."

"The party," wrote Mr. Girdlestone's correspondent, "*had been joined by persons of the most opposite sentiments,*" a condition which has historically characterized the Church of Rome's boasted UNITY. Moreover, the party aimed at SEPARATING THE CHURCH FROM THE STATE, *because the latter prevented the Romanizing party from being supreme, and from obtaining a purely Ecclesiastical Final Court of Appeal favourable to* their *de-*Protestantizing the Articles, Rubrics, Prayer Book, and Homilies of the Reformed Church of England, and our nation generally.

"Wicked men"—is the strong language used by the correspondent—"who are worse than Chushanishathaim of the Philistines," caused them to "groan under that heterogeneous unecclesiastical Parliament, *and they would not submit to its dictation."* *

With the aid of sympathizing laymen of their party, like their clerical leaders, acting *cautiously*, skilfully veiling their designs, and utilizing politicians and statesmen in all political parties, they have succeeded in *disintegrating Protestants both religiously and politically.* They have disestablished the Protestant Church in Ireland. They are *cautiously*

---

* The *Times*, of November 6th, 1890, gives a short summary of the charge delivered by the Bishop of Liverpool (Dr. Ryle) at his recent triennial visitation. His lordship made some weighty remarks of a most opportune character considering the reaction now going on in France against the many and serious evils, social and national, consequent on the over-labour inflicted on workmen, the infidelity, the demoralization, and other dark features resulting from the usual Continental Sunday. We read as follows:—

"In his triennial visitation charge, delivered on Tuesday in the Cathedral Church of St. Peter's, Liverpool, Bishop Ryle said that scepticism in England was the natural rebound from semi-Popery and superstition which many wise men had long predicted and expected. They must not be shaken in mind by it, or moved from their steadfastness, and they must hold fast to the doctrines of the Church as to the right observance of the Sabbath Day. They ought firmly and vigilantly to resist the persistent attempts frequently made to throw open places of amusement, aquariums, libraries, theatres, museums, picture-galleries, and the like, under the plausible pretence of 'affording recreation to the working classes.' He deeply regretted the assistance given to these attempts by laymen of high position and influence; but how any clergyman holding office in the Church of England, and reading the Fourth Commandment every Sunday to his congregation, could lend his aid to movements which must infallibly prevent the Sabbath being kept holy, if they succeeded, passed his understanding."

preparing the way for the disestablishment of
the Protestant Presbyterian Church in Scotland.
Then will come the turn of the Protestant
Church of England. Then, as Cardinal Manning well put it in the military language that
he so correctly uses, the crushing of the Protestant Churches of all denominations, generally,
will be simply " a war of detail," which *may* be
facilitated by an INVASION of our island, though,
to the delight of the Vatican, *pooh-poohed* by

With respect to the Ritualists and their lawless disregard of the
decisions against so many of their doctrines and practices, given
through the instrumentality of the CHURCH ASSOCIATION, by the
only Court known to English law, for the information and guidance of
all parties in our Church, the Bishop spoke in these words :—"So
long as those who thought the Courts incompetent declined to take any
steps to have better Courts created ; so long as it appeared agreed,
even in this Diocese, that no clergyman was ever to be called to account whatever he might teach and preach, and every one was to do
what was right in his own eyes ; so long as that law remained un-
repealed by which conscientious clergymen, declared guilty of
contumacy in doctrinal suits, might be sent to prison ; so long,"
he said, "as this miserable state of things continued, the present
condition of the Church seemed at first sight hopeless. But nothing
was impossible. He trusted they would always cultivate the
habit of treating Churchmen of other schools of thought than
their own with kindness, courtesy, and respect, giving them credit
for being as much in earnest as themselves, though they might
think them sadly mistaken. In any case they must not lightly forsake their mother, the Church of England. So long as they preserved
their Articles, Creed, and Prayer Book whole and unaltered, how could
they better their position by secession ? Where would they enjoy such
liberty, or find better prayers ? In what Communion would they find
so much good being done, in spite of the existence of much evil ?"

confident JOHN BULL—aided thereunto by the
Jesuits and blind Protestants—as an absurd and
ridiculous idea. Oh, for more men like the late
Dean McNeile and Canon Stowell, to apply,
under God's blessing, with their mighty
eloquence and unswerving faithfulness, the
imaginary but most telling story of " LITTLE
RED RIDING HOOD ! "

Mr. Keble and Mr. Newman allowed that, Mr.
Froude, " *though a Minister, was not a sound and
attached member of the English establishment ;
that he evaded the tests by a dry and literal
interpretation wording, and availed himself of
its influence and sustenance against itself.*"

The Bishop of Ossory, from whose charge in
1842 that extract is given in italics, proceeds
to expose the Jesuitical attempt of those clergymen to defend their friend from the charge of
being " an unfaithful minister of the Church."
Their answer—as his Lordship observes—"is
instructive, as illustrative of the view which the
[Tractarian] party took *of their obligations as
Ministers of the Anglican Church*, and of the
way and extent to which their relation to it
*was modified by their duties as Ministers of the
Church Catholic.*"

The Bishop gives the entire passage, of which the following is an extract :—"The view which the author [Mr. Froude] would take of his own position was probably this : that he was a minister, not of any human establishment, but of the one Holy Church Catholic, which has, in former times, been endowed by the piety of her members: that the State has but secured by law those endowments which it could not seize without sacrifice .... that [the Church's] ministers are in no way bound to throw themselves into the spirit of [various conditions calculated to bring the Church into bondage], rather are bound to keep themselves from the snare and guilt of them, and *to observe only such a literal acquiescence as is all that the law requires in any case, all that an external oppressor has a right to ask. Their loyalty is already engaged to* THE CHURCH CATHOLIC, and they cannot enter into the drift and intentions of her oppressors, without betraying her." *

By following so unprincipled a mode of excul-

---

* "The Judgment of the Bishops upon Tractarian Theology," by the Rev. W. Simcox Bricknell, M.A., Oxford, 1845 (pp. 65, 66, 67). The only word in italics is the word "*their.*"

C

pation from the obligation of observing solemn ordination engagements, how easy for Jesuits, and especially for men having that mark of THE APOSTASY, " consciences seared with a hot iron " (1 Tim. iv. 1-4), and that other mark, a " strong delusion " from Satan (2 Thess. ii. 7-12), to enter any Protestant Church, Episcopal or non-Episcopal, and deceive, seduce, and destroy souls !.

As the Bishop says, " When once this principle of the paramount duty of obedience to the Catholic Church had released a man from subjection to the authorities which God has set over him, talk of this kind, we know, would never be wanting to justify all that his own notions of Catholic views, or the notions of whatever little party, living or dead, he had chosen as the interpreter of the Catholic Church, might require him to say."

The defence set up by Mr. Newman and Mr. Keble for Mr. Froude, who, whilst a clergyman in our Church—was, as they themselves say—"not a sound and attached member " of her, but " evaded the tests," and " availed himself of its influence and sustenance against itself," is about on a par with Dr. Newman's attempted

defence of his "Tract XC.," explaining away the
Thirty-nine Articles, by what one of his own
party, the Rev. W. Ward, felt compelled to
stigmatize as a *"non-natural"* interpretation,
thus covering it with odium well-deserved,
though "exasperating" to Dr. Pusey. Dean
Goode, in his book on "Tract XC. Historically Refuted,"* quotes the avowed "main object
proposed" in the pamphlet, namely, " of defend-
ing, on *historical* grounds alone, the subscription
of those clergymen of our Church, or members of
the University (be they more or fewer), *who, in
subscribing, reserve to themselves the power of
holding all Roman Catholic doctrine* as distinct
on the one hand from popular perversions of it,
and, on the other, from the question of the
Papal jurisdiction " (Adv. p. 8). It was con-

---

* Hatchard & Co., 1866. The Dean notices "similar attempts in
former times in this country" to "Tract XC." "All such attempts,"
he remarks, were from "Catholic pens." One was by Christopher
Davenport, or, according to his Romish name, Francis a Sancta
Clara, in the days of Archbishop Laud, 1634. He took orders in the
Church of England. Dr. Waterland, in his remarks on Sancta Clara's
book, animadverts on his "professing his faith *in Protestant terms,
Popishly interpreted,*" showing that he "could not justly claim every
privilege of a Church of England man." (Goode, pp. 91, 119-131. See
also the remarks in the late Rev. Edward Bickersteth's charming
book, "The Promised Glory of the Church of Christ"—Seeley,
1844.)

C 2

tended that the Reformers couched their Formulary in language sufficiently Protestant in tone to satisfy the Reformers abroad, and sufficiently vague in expression to include the Catholics at home (*Ibid.* p. 9), whilst the tract asserted that "The Protestant confession was drawn up with the purpose of including Catholics, and now Catholics will not be excluded" ("Tract XC.," p. 83).

"A more painful misstatement,' observes Dean Goode, "and one, I will add, more obviously untrue and absurd to any one who is acquainted with the documents and history of the period, · could not be conceived" (pp. 6, 7).

Dr. Newman, himself, anticipated the condemnation of his interpretations, and actually refuted the misrepresentation given of the real object of the Articles, as just quoted. "It may be objected," he says, "that the tenor of the above explanations is anti-Protestant, whereas it is notorious that the Articles were drawn up by Protestants, and intended for the establishment of Protestantism ; accordingly, that it is an evasion of their meaning to give them any other than a Protestant drift, possible as it may be to do so grammatically, or in each separate part."*

Could self-condemnation be more complete? Of the subtle casuistry by which he endeavours to escape, the following sample may suffice :—"It is a *duty*,"† says Dr. Newman, "which *we owe both to the Catholic Church and to our own, to take our reformed confessions in the most Catholic sense they will* admit; *we have no duties towards their framers.*"

Again :—"In giving the Articles *a Catholic interpretation*, we *bring them into harmony*‡ *with the Book of Common Prayer.*"

---

* "Tract XC., with a Historical Preface," by the Rev. E. B. Pusey D.D., 1865 (p. 83).

† The word "*duty*" is italicized in Dr. Pusey's edition. The other italics are not in the original.

‡ So far from [Roman] "Catholic interpretation" being "in harmony with the Book of Common Prayer," as Dr. Pusey, Mr. Newman, and other deceivers have laboured to make out, one of the greatest proofs of the emphatic Protestantism of our Prayer Book consists in the fact that our Reformers *expurgated* the Liturgy from the idolatries and superstitions of the Church of Rome's Offices. This is amply proved in the splendid defence of the Church of England's Articles, Liturgy, and Homilies in the late Mr. Isaac Taylor's "ANCIENT CHRISTI-ANITY" (4th ed., 1844, vol. ii.).

It is the fatal ignorance of our Laity, that leaves them at the mercy of Romanizing bishops and clergymen.

"As to the LITURGY of the Church," says Mr. Taylor, "it is Protestant, not by protesting against Popish and ancient superstitions, but by silently eschewing them—a better protest, surely !" . . . .

"The uninformed—albeit devout—attendant upon the worship of

"The "Oxford Triumvirate,* Mr. NEWMAN,
Dr. PUSEY, and Mr. KEBLE," thought it their
DUTY, then, to poison and transform our "*reformed* formularies" with "the most Catholic
[*i.e., Roman* Catholic] sense" possible.

So, the Apostle Paul, whilst in his unconverted state, as "the natural man," who "re-
ceiveth not the things of the Spirit of God :
for they are foolishness to him : neither can he
know them, because they are spiritually dis-
cerned" (1 Cor. ii. 13, 14 ; Rom. viii. 5-9),
though, as a Pharisee, he was one of the most
religious and ascetic of men, and, outwardly,
"touching the righteousness which is in the
law, blameless" (Phil. iii. 4-6), thought it his

---

the English. Church knows the service simply in its absolute
merits ; but he would regard it in another manner if he distinctly
knew *from what associations* this 'form of sound words' has been
rescued, and from what dregs it has been purified !" (p. 490).

In another place he says, "Is not the Church of England, then, as
truly Protestant in its omissions, as in its protests ?   It is Protestant
in its loud and righteous indignation, and Protestant, not less, in its
contemptuous silence ; Protestant when it denounces Rome as Antichrist ; and Protestant—and even with a deeper emphasis—when it
consigns to oblivion the errors of the more ancient apostasy " (p. 489).

Is the Black Rubric on Kneeling, at the end of the Communion
Service, " in harmony " with the Mass ?

* See "A Second Plea for the Reformed Church," by the Rev.
Charles Bird, M.A., F.L.S. (Hatchard, 1843.)   He was Chancellor of
Lincoln Cathedral, 1859.

DUTY " to do many things contrary to the name
of Jesus of Nazareth," and that, like the spiritually mesmerized or "hypnotized" laity ex-
ecuting the imperious will of the Church of
Rome, "drunken with the blood of the saints"
(Rev. xvii. 1-6), [and ready to be so inebriated
again, if only befooled Protestants enable her
to be so] the zealous Apostle imagined that he
"OUGHT" to "shut up many of the saints in
prison, having received authority from the chief
priests ; and when they were put to death, he
gave his voice against them," and "compelled
them to blaspheme" (Acts xxvi. 4-19), as
Popish murderers have cruelly tortured and
slain multitudes of Christ's faithful witnesses
for not having consented to the "blasphemous
fables and dangerous deceits" of their polytheistic "gods many" in their many MASS
wafers.   How sorrowfully did he afterwards
bewail his having been "a blasphemer, and a
persecutor, and injurious !" (1 Tim. i. 12-15).

But the authorities at Oxford had *their* duty
also to carry out. So, the Hebdomadal Board
met and considered "Tract XC.," and they
passed the following resolution :—

"RESOLVED, That the modes of interpreta-

tion, such as are suggested in the said Tract,
evading, rather than explaining, the sense of
the Thirty-nine Articles " [the very opinion, as
we have seen, anticipated by Mr. Newman
himself], "and reconciling subscription to them,
with the adoption of errors which they were
designed to counteract, defeat the object, and
are inconsistent with the observance of the
above-mentioned STATUTES."*

Now, why was that dishonest Tract sent
forth ? An unexceptional witness shall tell us.
Mr. KEBLE, in his letter to The Hon. Mr.
Justice Coleridge on " The Case of Catholic
Subscription to the Thirty-nine Articles,"
appended to Dr. Pusey's edition of the Tract,
and not much inferior in casuistry to the
Tract itself, thus states the very remarkable
why and wherefore of its publication.

" The chief ground, indeed," says Mr. Keble,
"has been already stated by Mr. Newman, *viz.*, its
being known as a fact, that *persons imbued with
Catholic principles, and desirous of carrying out*
in good faith the views which they seemed to
themselves to have learned from sacred anti-

---

* Bricknell, p. 668.

quity," [but ignoring that part of it which preceded the enslavement and corruption of the British Church by the Papacy] " WERE IN SOME POINTS STAGGERED BY THE TONE AND WORDING OF THE ARTICLES." *

They were, indeed, fearfully staggered, as one of their agonized number will presently tell us.

The fact is, the " poisoning " " conspirators " had to deal with " persons " of various kinds and degrees of conscientiousness, love of truth, sense of honour, and fear of accountability " before the Judgment Seat of Christ."

This is pointed out in a very instructive article on " Catholic Revival in the Church of England," which appeared in the *Union Review* of 1867. It is quoted in " Tract LXXII.," published by the Church Association, from which the following extracts are taken :—

" The writer, who is an avowed Ritualist, is, be it remembered, not only in communion, but in perfect sympathy with his correspondent, the Roman Catholic priest, in point of doctrine and ritual."

---

* Italics and capitals not in the original.

In illustration of the different degrees of rapidity with which the Romanizers were able to *educate up* into Romanism, and cajole and captivate "flattered Churchmen" in our congregations, the Ritualist thus writes to his friend :—

"It happens that the churches in which *Catholic principles* are being carried out* present no uniformity at present, but are all at

---

* Since the Oxford "Movement," "the vestries," says Dr. Maurice, "have not been constructed as heretofore, but rather after Popish models, with a door on the outside for the purpose of allowing them to go round the church, and re-enter in processional way."—"The Ritualists, or Non-National Catholics," by the Rev. Peter Maurice, D.D. (Int. p. v.).

Processions, with Romanistic banners, having a large cross on them, and crosses carried on the top of a staff abound. Now, the *cross* is the special *mark* or "*symbol* of the Romish worship." It was also "used in the Babylonian mysteries," and "was applied by Paganism to the same magic purposes, and was honoured with the same honours as by the Church of Rome. To say that Rome's superstitious feeling for the sign of the cross . . . . ever grew out of the saying of Paul, 'God forbid, that I should glory save in the Cross of our Lord Jesus Christ,' *that is, in the doctrine of Christ crucified*, is a mere absurdity, a shallow subterfuge, a pretence. . . . . That which is now called the Christian cross, was originally no Christian emblem at all, but was the mystic Tau of the Chaldeans and Egyptians—the true original form of the letter T—the initial of the name of Tammur—which, in Hebrew, radically the same as ancient Chaldee, as found on coins, was formed as in No. 1 of the accompanying woodcut (fig. 43), and in Etruria and Coptic, as in Nos. 2 and 3."—Quoted from "The Two Babylons," by the Rev. Alexander Hislop. (Houlston & Wright, 3rd ed., 1862, pp. 288 and 289.)

See also, "The Cross, Heathen and Christian," by the Rev. Mourant Brook, M.A. (3rd ed., Elliot Stock, 1879.)

different stages in the progress of emersion from Protestantism to Catholicism. The rapidity of this progressive change will, of course, vary according to the nature and degree of the obstructions it may meet with. . . . . On an average, perhaps, we may say it requires ten years. It would, I fear, take too long to give you a sketch *of the various steps by which such a* TRANSFORMATION *is effected.* You can picture to yourself what a task it would be to *transform* one of your Lutheran churches *into a building fitted in all respects for a Catholic system of service,** and its congregation into a

---

* Amongst other things, we see altarwise "structures," shaming our Church's "*honest tables*" alone suited to a *Supper*. We have unlawful "altars," with steps leading up to them, favoured unhappily by the strange omission in the Injunctions for the removal of the *stone altars* to include *the steps*. Of this Jesuitical Romanizers have taken advantage.

We have also unlawful *retables*, with crosses and flowers *appearing* to form part of the table, in resemblance of a Popish altar. But, as placing a cross, &c., *on* the table would be contrary to law, and would expose bishops and clergy to punishment, they place the forbidden objects *on a line with* or *just above* the table—thus, in effect, breaking the law in its spirit, but escaping its penalties.

Yet, perhaps, on any Sunday, such bishops and clergy will gravely enforce on the scandalized laity the duty of "*avoiding all appearance of evil*," or the Christian duty of avoiding *equivocation*, and the *acting* as well as *speaking* a lie !

Such lamentable things are increasingly seen from John o' Groat's to the Land's End, including Truro Cathedral, and too many churches in Cornwall.

body of well-instructed and devout Catholic worshippers."

The harrowing effects of such "transforming steps" in persons subjected to them are shown in a most vivid and deeply-affecting way in a remarkable tract, written by one of the victims, and entitled, " The Morality of Tractarianism : A Letter from one of the People to one of the Clergy."* (London : W. Pickering, 1850.) This tract excited a profound sensation—and no wonder. The processes employed by the clerical "wolves in sheep's clothing" (Matt. vii., 15-23), with the tortures thereby inflicted mentally and morally, and only comparable to those inflicted [beyond words to express] by too many Roman Catholic directors and confessors,† may, to some extent, be gathered from the following extracts :—

After remarking on the sore perplexities caused by the opposite doctrines drawn from "the same authorities," by " the commanders " of the

---

* The pamphlet was put forth from "some observations in Mr. Maskell's Second Letter on the position of the High Church Party." Mr. Maskell was Chaplain to Bishop Phillpotts, but seceded to the Church of Rome.

† See that deeply interesting and most instructive small volume, written with great tact, delicacy, and force, by Mrs. Richardson, and entitled, "Personal Experience of Roman Catholicism," 6th edition

Movement, amongst other things telling the rank
and file that " the decision of the judicial committee is not binding," and then by "another ingenious reasoning, making it as clear as day-
light, that unless something is done within, as
it were, four-and-twenty hours [they] stand
committed to heresy," the writer adds, " *We
fall back on common sense, on honest conscience,
and a love of truth*, and perhaps they are likely
to be as safe guides *as the great learning dis-
played to prove contraries.*"

Then, alluding to " that much vaunted system"
for " the revival of Catholic opinions within the
Church of England, which is called Tractarianism by its enemies, and Catholicism by its
friends," he says, "*To many of us who have
lived under its shadow, and trusted in it, there
has been all along a secret doubt about its per-
manency and truth, an uneasiness whether it*

(Morgan & Scott.)   The introduction is by the Rev. Charles B.
Taylor, Rector of Ipswich. With Mrs. Richardson's book compare—
"Sisterhoods in the Church of England," by Margaret Goodman.
(3rd edition, Smith, Elder & Co., 1864.)
"The Priest, The Woman, and The Confessional," by Père
Chiniquy. (W. T. Gibson, 5th edition, 1878.)
"The Confessional," by the Rev. Hobart Seymour. (1870.)
"Nunnery Life in the Church of England," by Sister Mary Agnes,
O.S.B.   Introduction by the Rev. W. Lancelot Holland, M.A.
(Hodder & Stoughton, 1890.)

were all it seemed; a question, in fact, whether it were human or divine."

Alluding to " the laity generally," he remarks, " It cannot be said that the uneasiness I speak of has had its cause in their not thoroughly believing the doctrines alluded to. It may rather be attributed *to their natural habit of judging questions simply from their moral bearing, apart from all argument and casuistry, and from the irresistible suspicion which arises in such plain minds,* that however true the doctrines sought to be revived, however necessary to salvation right faith in them may be, still, that Tractarianism, or the attempt *to revive* them among ourselves WITHOUT ANY CHANGE IN OUR FORMULARIES, OR IN OUR OWN POSITION AS A CHURCH,—HAS A MORAL EVIL IN IT, A TAINT AND STAIN OF UNTRUTHFULNESS, WHICH MAKES HONEST AND GOOD HEARTS SHRINK FROM IT. It strikes men like these as something which, under the guise of truth, *has in it the seeds of evasion* and dishonour. . . . . We are wont," he says, " to speak of the English character as straightforward and honest, even to bluntness, and to attach the idea of intellectual subtlety almost exclusively to more southern nations. But never, surely, was there any nation that has given such proof of this last kind of mental power as England, by the growth of Tractarianism."

Evidently alluding to the remedy for Catholicized but staggering minds in "Tract XC.,"the writer says,"Our teachers . . . . having all previously given their *ex animo* consent to articles whose obvious intention, to unlearned minds, was to *oppose* such doctrines, does accustom us to the principle of ingenious interpretation. But it did not remove the difficulty of having to believe certain truths, *and afterwards to try and believe that his Church teaches them.*"

"If, then," he remarks, "we first acknowledge that the only way of holding such truths in the English Church is by the use of non-natural interpretation, and then also acknowledge that these truths are the heritage of the people, not the exclusive privilege of the educated classes, we must begin by spreading the spirit of casuistry among our village schools and labourers' cottages ; we must make our wives and

---

* The words " *ex animo* " and " *oppose*" are in italics.

daughters students in scholastic niceties, and in a degree we have done so.

"Where we have not, we have left them Protestants. Where we have, we have made them false."

In fervent terms he relates how "very slowly, perhaps, and by degrees, they came to receive" in the Lord's Supper, the Romish dogma of 'A Presence, a Real Presence, a Sacrifice—adoration—communion.' With keenest anguish he speaks of their irrepressible and 'terrible doubt' as to 'whether our own Church and Prayer Book really taught all this.' . . . . Our teachers," he adds, "insist that we are wrong, and—strange as it may seem—that all which we have learnt *is* in the Prayer Book! Take the Eucharist, for example. It is very true (we are told) that transubstantiation is said to overthrow the nature of a sacrament, *but we are not called on to sign the Articles ;** therefore, it cannot concern us that the doctrine of the sacrifices of Masses† is called

---

* From the above sentence, we may infer, apparently, that the writer was a layman.

† Mr. Newman, in "Tract XC." on Article XXXI., endeavoured to make out that, "Here the sacrifice of the *Mass* is not spoken of, in which the special question of doctrine would be introduced ; but the

a blasphemous fable and dangerous deceit. *It is true there is an alarming rubric at the end of the Communion Service,* warning men that they are not to adore, and that our dearest faith is idolatry ; but though the ' thing to be abhorred of all faithful Christians ' is the very life of our life, there is a something about the word ' natural ' in the sentence, which is to help us through ; how, we scarcely know, but we are told not to fear : we may believe, and we may adore. Spite of the words looking No, their real, genuine, honest meaning must be

---

' sacrifice of *Masses*'*—certain observances, for the most part private and solitary." He actually refers to Bishop Burnet as supporting that sophistical distinction, equal to any "distinguo" of the schoolmen.

Now Bishop Burnet flatly condemns such an interpretation in the extract, as quoted by Mr. Newman himself. The Bishop says, in striking confirmation of the statements of Mr. Isaac Taylor in his "Ancient Christianity," " It were easy, from all the rituals of the ancients, to show *that they had none of those ideas that are now in the Roman Church. . . . . So far were they from* the many altars in every church, and *the many masses* [sic] at every altar, *that are now in the Roman Church,* they did not know what *solitary masses* [sic] were, without a communion. All the liturgies and all the writings of ancients are as express in the matter as possible." As will be seen, the Bishop witnessed against *all* the *novelties* of the Roman Church.

Moreover, it has been pointed out, in refutation of Mr. Newman's gloss, that the heading of the Article is, " Of *the* ONE oblation of Christ finished on the Cross."

---

* In the original, the words " Mass," " Masses," "the many masses," and " solitary masses," are in italics.

D

Yes. And we submit; but nevermore is the
Tremendous Sacrifice what it was to us in the
early days of faith. . . . . THE SHRINE IS
EMPTY; THE DIVINITY GONE. WE TREAD THE
AISLE WITH FALTERING STEPS, *trying to do as
we are bid, and* TO DROWN OUR DOUBTS WITH
CLEVER PREVARICATIONS."

Surely, no comment is needed on such deeply
affecting, such harrowing outpourings. The
honesty as well as the anguish of the writer are
stamped on every page. At its close he says,
" One side or the other, only no more compro-
mise : we have groaned under that burden long
enough ; no longer will we submit to the dis
honour of a constant subterfuge."

No marvel to find the writer saying, " If "
[the Roman Mass " treasure " is] not within the
fold of our English Mother, we will seek it elsewhere. . . . . *And so it comes to pass that
simple minds begin to think of* ROME."

As some aid towards " reading between the
lines " in some of the foregoing citations, the
following peeps from Dean GOODE's valuable
" Case as it is," giving the opinions of the Tract-
ators from their own published writings, may be
found useful. Alluding, apparently, to their so-

called " Church-principles," Mr. Newman, in his Letter to the Bishop of Oxford, laments that "persons of practised intellects, with or without unfriendly motives, are ever drawing out the ultimate conclusions in which our principles result, and forcing us to affirm or deny what we would *fain not consider or not pronounce upon.*" "Which," says the Dean, "is as much as to say, It is very inconvenient that men should be enabled to see at once whither we want to lead them, because we wish to lead them on unconsciously."

Mr. Newman recommended what, in theological parlance, is called "*economy.*" As the Dean says, "It will be best in Mr. Newman's own words," taken from his "Arians of the Fourth Century."

"The Alexandrian father" (Clement), says Mr. Newman, "who has already been referred to, *accurately describes the rules which should guide the Christian in speaking and acting economically.* . . . . He both thinks and speaks the truth, EXCEPT WHEN CONSIDERATION IS NECESSARY, AND THEN, AS A PHYSICIAN FOR THE GOOD OF HIS PATIENTS, HE WILL BE FALSE, OR UTTER A FALSEHOOD, AS THE SOPHISTS SAY. . . . . Nothing, however, but *his neighbour's good* will lead him to do this. *He gives himself up for the Church,"* &c.

"Upon this passage," says the Dean, "I will not trust myself to make any remark" (p. 8).

Was it in accordance with the science of *economy*, and because he had "given himself up for *the* CHURCH," as every blinded and spiritually coerced Romanist is expected to do, that Mr. Newman—as afterwards confessed in writing by him—published in lectures and articles the strongest protests against the "system of Rome," because the "conspirators" —to use his own words—" FOUND IT NECESSARY FOR THEIR POSITION," in order "TO REPEL THE CHARGE OF ROMANISM"?*

In his "Retractation," after his open secession to the Church of Rome, he wrote a letter of "explanation" to the editor of *The Conservative Journal*, dated December, 1842.

Here are some extracts from it :—

"It is true," he says, "that I have at various times, in writing against the Roman system, used not merely arguments, about

---

* The witty Dean Sydney Smith, in his terse and telling language, is said to have characterized Tractarianism as *Posture* and *Imposture*.

which I am not here speaking, but what reads
like declamation. For instance, in 1833,"
[when the Tractarians opened their campaign]
" in the *Lyra Apostolica*, I called it a 'lost
Church.'

" 2. Also, in 1883, I spoke of the ' Papal
Apostasy' in a work upon the Arians," [above
quoted]. . . . .

" 5. In 1834, I said, in a magazine :—' The
spirit of old Rome has risen again in its former
place, and has evidenced its identity by its
works. It has possessed the Church there
planted,* as an evil spirit might seize the de-
moniacs of primitive times, and makes her

---

* How wonderfully condensed, how true, and how deeply impressive
is the sketch of the Church of Rome's paganism, her "cruelty,"
"craft," "ambition," "its forced celibacy within," and "its persecutions without," "its craft and its falsehoods," "its deceitful
deeds and lying wonders," [its *economy ?*] &c., &c. Mr. Newman,
all the while, was only "*transformed*" into the *appearance* of a true
Protestant. He allowed the hoodwinked bishops, clergy, and laity
of our Church, and the public at large, to believe that such were
his own convictions, or those of *the Tractarians*. Not at all. He
said to himself, "I am not speaking my own words; I am but following almost a *consensus* of the divines of my Church," namely, the
Church of England, of which he was *outwardly* a minister !—Read in
that light, is there not a fearful sardonic irony in the apparently unconscious self-application of so much of the picture of his own acts !

Was CARDINAL NEWMAN really entitled to the glowing eulogies
recently devoted to him, and especially to his " honesty," not only
in the political papers, nor even in certain Church papers, but also in
Nonconformist journals ?

speak words which are not her own. In the corrupt Papal system, we have the very cruelty, the craft, and the ambition of the republic ; its cruelty in its unsparing sacrifice of the happiness and virtue of individuals to a phantom of public expediency, in its forced celibacy within and its persecutions without, its craft in its falsehoods, its deceitful deeds and lying wonders, and its grasping ambition in the very structure of its policy, in its assumption of universal dominion; old Rome is still alive; nowhere have its eagles lighted, but it still claims the sovereignty under another pretence. The Roman Church I will not blame, but pity—*she is, as I have said, spell-bound, as if by an evil spirit ; she is in thraldom.*"

As regards the last sentence, not italicized in the original, it may be found most impressive by true Christians, sincerely and earnestly imploring the Holy Spirit's teaching, in the name of Jesus Christ, *carefully to compare* 2 Thess. ii. 3-12 ; John xvii. 12—vi. 70, 71 ; 2 Cor. xi. 1-3, 13-15 ; Matt. vii. 15-23 ; 1 Tim. iv. 1-5 ; 2 Tim. i. 1-13 ; Matt. xxiv. 5, 22-28 ; Rev. ii. 2, xiii., xvii., xviii ; Dan. vii.

Those Scriptures display a wonderful pro-

phetic delineation of the Church of Rome's
character and history, in measure applicable to
Tractarians and to Ritualists. Should it not
cause *thoughtful* students to examine *with special
care* the Scripture and History credentials of
ecclesiastics claiming APOSTOLIC SUCCESSION,
exclusive and peculiar Apostolic power and
authority ?*

---

* In connection with the above extracts it is instructive—at any rate,
to us of the laity—to read carefully Bishop Jewel's works, and, in particular, his Exposition of St. Paul's 2nd Epistle to the Thessalonians
(chap. ii. 3, 12). No wonder that the Tractarian leaders branded
him as "an irreverent Dissenter." Do not "almost a *consensus*" of
the great divines and faithful witnesses of our Church since the Reformation, with those of sister non-episcopal Churches, deserve the
same honourable reproach ? St. Paul did not escape it (Acts xxiv.).
As regards the essentially *heathen* origin of much in the Church of
Rome, and as showing her departures from Holy Scripture and primitive antiquity, the following works afford valuable and interesting
information :—

1. "A Letter from Rome," by Dr. Conyers Middleton, 1812, and
later editions.

2. "The Two Babylons," by Rev. Alexander Hislop. (3rd edition,
Houlston & Wright, 1812.)

3. "The Catacombs of Rome," by the Rev. W. H. Withrow, M.A.
(Hodder & Stoughton, 1888.) This valuable book is well illustrated.

4. "Roma Antiqua et Recens." (Reprinted from the edition of
1732, Elliot Stock, 1889.)

5. "The Catacombs at Rome," by Benjamin Scott, F.R.A.S.,
Chamberlain of the City of London. (Morgan & Scott, 4th edition).
Most interesting and instructive, and full of illustrations, of Chris-
tian inscriptions, &c.

6. Also, Bishop Christopher Wordsworth's learned and most convincing little book, "Union with Rome. Is not the Church of Rome
the Babylon of the Book of Revelation?" (Rivington's, 8th edition,
1874.)

Mr. Newman quotes many more of his utterances, and then makes this astounding confession :—

" If you ask me how an individual could venture, not simply to hold, but to publish* such views of a communion so ancient, so widespreading, so fruitful in saints, I answer, that I said to myself, ' *I am not speaking my own words*, I am but following almost a *consensus* of the divines of my Church. They have ever used the strongest language against Rome, even the most able and learned of them. *I wish to throw myself into their system. While I say what they say, I am safe.* Such views, too, *are necessary for our position.*' Yet I have reason to fear still that such language is to be ascribed, in no small measure, to an impetuous temper, a hope of approving myself to persons' respect, *and a wish to repel the charge of Romanism.*"†

---

* Blind, implicit obedience, called "holy obedience" to "*the* Church," that is, to her priesthood, is a fundamental and inflexible rule in the Church of Rome. It is obedience to the supreme will of a human superior, who, in effect, usurps the place of God and of His will expressed in His written Word. Rome forbids her dupes to read the Bible for themselves, and without the interpretation of the priest, for fear "the light should reprove " [or convict] "the Church " of false teaching (John iii. 16-21). Roman Catholics may "*hold*," but may not "*publish*" truth injurious to " the Church."

† " Consensus " is the only word in italics in the original.

Any one who loves "Truth for its own sake," and advocates "saying what we mean, and meaning what we say;" any one who, whilst overpowered by the display of great dialectic skill, and of dazzling verbal oratory, yet prefers that eloquence which is defined as "Truth spoken with simplicity;" any such person, as the writer thinks, will rise up with admiration of the truthful and transparent nature of the Rev. Charles Kingsley's mind and method of controversy, as evidenced in his pamphlet entitled, "What, then, does Dr. Newman mean?"* in reply to the publication by the latter of a correspondence between Mr. Kingsley and himself.

. That publication was caused by an article from Mr. Kingsley in *Macmillan's Magazine* for January, 1864.

The extracts given in the latter's reply are in startling and painful accordance with the illustrations of Dr. Newman's notions of truth, simplicity, and honour, quoted in these pages from the writings of Dr. O'Brien, Bishop of Ossory, Dean Goode, and Dr. Newman's work on the Arians.

Mr. Kingsley says, "I deliberately and advisedly made use of these words :—

---

* Macmillan & Co., 1864.

" Truth, for its own sake, had never been a
virtue with the Roman Clergy. Father Newman informs us that it need not, and, on the
whole, ought not to be ; that cunning is the
weapon. . . . . This accusation I based upon a
considerable number of Dr. Newman's writings,
and especially on a sermon entitled ' Wisdom
and Innocence.' "

Dr. Newman wrote in strong but courteous
terms to Messrs. Macmillan & Co., complaining
of this language as a slander.   Mr. Kingsley at
once took the responsibility on himself, and
wrote to Dr. Newman.

The latter appended to the correspondence
" certain reflections in which," says Mr.
Kingsley, " he attempted to convict me of not
having believed the accusation which I had
made."*   Of the nature of that attempt, he
thus writes, " Dr. Newman tries, by cunning
sleight-of-hand logic, to prove that I did not
believe the accusation when I made it. Therein
he is mistaken.   I did believe it ; and I believed, also, his indignant denial."   But, " now
that Dr. Newman has become (one must needs
suppose) suddenly, and since the 1st of

---

* P. 7.

February, 1864, a convert to the economic views of St. Alfonso de Liguori and his compeers, I am henceforth in doubt and fear, as much as an honest man can be, concerning every word Dr. Newman may write. How can I tell that I shall not be the dupe of some cunning equivocation, of one of the three kinds laid down as permissible by the blessed St. Alfonso de Liguori and his pupils even when confirmed with an oath, because ' then we do not deceive our neighbour, but allow him to deceive himself' ? * . . . . It is admissible, therefore, to use words and sentences which have a double signification, and leave the hapless hearer to take which of them he may choose. What proof have I, then, that by ' *mean* it ! I never *said* it !' Dr. Newman does not signify, ' did not say it, but I did [query *not* ?] mean it ' ? " †

The illustrations given by Mr. Kingsley of Dr. Newman's proficiency in the science of ECONOMY are very saddening. " He has committed," says the former, " on the very title-page of his pamphlet an ' economy ' which some men

---

* I quote from Scavini, tom. ii., p. 232, of the Paris edition, and from Neyraguet, p. 141, two compendiums of Liguori which are (or were lately) used, as I have every reason to believe—one at Oscott, the other at Maynooth.

† P. 44.

will consider a very serious offence. He has
there stated that the question is 'Whether Dr.
Newman teaches that truth is no virtue.' . . . .
He has economized the very four words of my
accusation, which makes it at least a reasonable
one ; namely, ' *For its own sake.*' I never said
what he makes me say, or anything like it. I
never was inclined to say so."*

Curiously enough, as in the case of his "Tract
XC.," Dr. Newman anticipated what might be
said against his "method of teaching" by " the
world." "What wonder," remarks Mr. Kingsley,
" if they said of him (as he so naively in one of
his letters expresses his fear that they will say
again), ' Dr. Newman has the skill of a great
master of verbal fence, who knows as well as any
man living how to insinuate a doctrine without
committing himself to it ' ? If he told the world,
as he virtually does in this sermon, ' I know
that my conduct looks like cunning, but it is
only the " arts " of the defenceless,' what wonder
if the world answered, ' No, it is what it means.
That is just what we call cunning ; a habit of
mind which, once indulged, is certain to go from
bad to worse, till the man becomes—like too

* P. 43.

many of the mediæval clergy who indulged in it—utterly untrustworthy?"*

Mr. Newman and Mr. Keble held that "our Communion Service is 'a judgment on the Church;'" and Mr. Newman, writing to Dr. Fausset, said that "our Reformers, in not adopting 'the Canon of the Mass,' which is a 'sacred and precious monument of the Apostles, mutilated the tradition of 1,500 years,' and 'our present condition is a judgment on us for what they did.'"† Mr. Keble, in his preface to Hooker, laments that, our Reformers "have 'given up altogether the ecclesiastical tradition regarding certain *very material* points in the celebration, if not in the doctrine, of the Holy Eucharist.'"‡

Such is an imperfect sketch of a system which, for years past, has been seeking in its principles and its practices to exhibit its steadily developing desires after a resumption

---

* P 17:

† Mr. Newman hesitates not to assert that the "Canon of the Mass" is a "monument of the Apostles." Is that a specimen of *economy?* Mr. Froude advised that the name "Liturgy of St. Peter" be "substituted for the obnoxious phrase '*Mass-Book*,' a hint not thrown away" (Bricknell, p. 63). Dr. F. G. Lee has preferred the name "Directorium Anglicanum."

‡ "Case as it is," p. 33.

of an "historical continuity" with the Church of Rome. Yet there are persons within our Church who would persuade the confiding laity that such a system is *true* "Anglicanism,"despite the adverse witness of history, and the more primitive antiquity of the independent British Church ; and despite, also, of the exceedingly strong testimony, quoted in these pages, of Mr. Newman, chief of the Tractarians, to the noble refutations of Popery evinced—to use his own words—by " almost a *consensus* of the divines " of our Reformed Church.*

We have now to consider the assertion that, "*Protestantism* is destructive, and not construct-ive, and *is powerless as a moral force.*"

Therefore, consistently and logically according to that teaching, Romanism ought to be vastly superior to Protestantism as a moral force.

But if there is one thing more certain than another, is it not this—namely, that—to pursue the inquiry no further—the history of Europe

---

* The chief works of our eminent Protestant bishops and divines, from the days of the Reformation, are included in the 56 vols. of the Parker Society. Also in the "Preservatives from Popery," edited by Bishop Gibson. Dr. Willett's "Synopsis Papismi" includes most valuable testimony from other Protestant Churches. An excellent collection of the works of our Reformers has been published by the Religious Tract Society.

during the past thousand years, and especially since the days of the Reformation, entirely negatives the assertion in question, and, whether it be socially, politically, or nationally, proves the very reverse?

Of course, a full description of so complicated a question would fill the pages of a large volume, if not more than one. There must also, as a preliminary, be a mutual understanding as to what is to be understood by the expressions "Romanism" and "Protestantism."

We live in days when words and statements are transformed into totally different things, owing to alien meanings foisted into them, enabling verbal and theological conjurors to produce wonderful illusions before the uninitiated. We laymen, in particular, stand in great need of some helpful glossary for our protection. Take a few of the words in question.

1. "Catholic," used to signify *Roman* Catholic, without acknowledging such to be the intended meaning, or to signify what Romanists, Tractarians, and Ritualists deceivingly labour to persuade the laity is the real teaching of the Church of England, despite the contrary teaching of her Articles, which, says the Declar-

ation, "do contain her true doctrine agreeably to God's Word," her homilies, and her rubrics.

2. "Church Principles,"* alleged to exemplify the real principles of Holy Scripture, and of *the oldest and purest* " primitive antiquity," whereas such is far from the truth. Moreover, Tractarians and Ritualists not infrequently allow themselves a "reservation" of the *Roman Catholic sense* of the word "Church" when united to "Principles."

3. "Priest," which in our Prayer Book means simply "presbyter writ short," and *never* means *a vicarious sacrificing and mediatorial* priest, such as the priests of the Greek and the Roman Churches. Hence the bitter animosity of Mr. Newman, Mr. Froude, and others, as we have seen, against our Articles, our Communion Service, and the rubric on kneeling at the end of that Service. Too many of our laity, and a still larger number of Nonconformists, have been mystified and led astray into a false belief that our Church and her Prayer Book sanctioned that unwarrantable misinterpretation of the

---

* On "Church Principles," see specially "The Kingdom of Christ," by Archbishop Whately, and Dean Goode's invaluable work, "The Divine Rule of Faith and Practice." It deals, amongst other things, in his usual masterly way with Mr. Keble's work on Tradition.

true meaning intended by the mere *word*
" priest."

If every *word* susceptible of being perverted by disingenuous and casuistical adversaries must therefore be expunged from prayer books and hymn books, what would become of such words as " Church," " truth," " faith, " " Lord's Supper " (made to be synonymous with the Popish Mass, and the kindred " Eucharistic Sacrifice " of Tractarians and Ritualists), "Scripture," made by Romanists to include the Apocrypha, and placed on a level with reputed *unwritten* truths or traditions and interpretations of ecclesiastics, " making the Word of God of none effect " ? (Matt. xv.)

4. " Calvinists," used ignorantly by many, and by some maliciously, often applied to thoroughly Evangelical and Protestant clergy and laity, who are abused as " bigots," " ultra-Protestants," and by other names, by Romish foes, and by worldly men of no fixed and duly operative Christian principles. Such men seek " not to give offence " by standing up for the truth, but to " make things pleasant " to every one, at whatever cost to the cause of Christ, or to the welfare of souls. Whether from " the fear of

E

man which brings a snare," or from worldly self-
interest, such men shrink from suffering for
Christ's sake.   Our Lord spoke strongly of men
"receiving honour one of another, and not
seeking the honour that cometh from God only."
This they did, because " they had not the love
of God in them " (John v. 41-47).   As the late
Dr. Cunningham has shown in his " Historic
Theology," and as was shown some time ago in
some valuable letters published by a layman in
the *Record*, the doctrines of God's free and
unmerited grace, which are by some men called
" Calvinism," might as well be called " Augus-
tinism," or rather " Paulinism."

5. " Dissenter," which is made to signify not
merely conscientious Protestant Nonconformists, but also such faithful and consistent
Evangelical clergy and laity of our Church as,
through grace, have been delivered from that
" fear of man " which worketh a snare; who are
more solicitous to be good *Christians* in the sight
of God our Saviour, than to be esteemed good
" *Churchmen* " or good *party politicians* in
the opinions of men ; who. through the
power of the Holy Spirit, are ready to
bear contempt, depreciation, ridicule, and other

ill-usage for Christ's sake ; and who, from supreme regard for the Word of God, *conform* to it, and *dissent* from Popery and Ritualism. Contrariwise, Ritualists *dissent* from our Church's Scriptural and Protestant teaching, and lawlessly refuse to *conform* either to it or to the decisions against Ritualism by the only judicial Court known to English law—a law subject to which our bishops and our clergy voluntarily entered on their ordination engagements. Consequently, the " Dissenters " and " Nonconformists," against whom we find ourselves compelled especially to protest, are those who are *within*, but not *of*, our Protestant Church.

By Tractarians, even our great Bishop Jewel, whose famous Apology [or Defence] of the Church of England against her Romanist foes used to be carefully chained up as a treasure with the Bible in English within our churches, for the enlightenment of all ranks and classes— even he is bitterly abused in Froude's "Remains," and in other Tractarian writings, and is pilloried as "an irreverent dissenter," probably on account of his crushing exposure of the unscriptural, unhistorical, and fallacious charges of

his Jesuit adversary, M. Harding. In particular, whereas the validity of the orders in our
Reformed Church was assailed as lacking true
APOSTOLICAL SUCCESSION,* the Bishop quietly
advised his opponent first to make sure—if he
could do so—of the *bonâ fide* historical succession of bishops in his own Church. He shows, as
do other ecclesiastical writers and historians,
that the Church of Rome *cannot possibly be
sure of the historical warrant for the first three
links of her imaginary personal succession.* In
many ways, even on orthodox Episcopal principles, has that pretentious claim been completely vitiated and nullified in the history of
the Church of Rome.

The fact is in reality incontrovertible, that,
no form of Church Government whatever,

---

* On the subject of "Apostolical Succession," compare—1. Bishop
Lightfoot on Colossians, containing his dissertation on the Christian
Ministry ; 2. The Rev. Dr. Jacob's "Ecclesiastical Polity of the New
Testament ;" 3. "Whose are the Fathers?" by Rev. Dr. John Harrison (Longmans, Green, & Co., 1867) ; 4. "The Growth of Church
Institutions, and Organization of Early Christian Churches," by the
Rev. Dr. Hatch ; 5. Archbishop Whately's "Kingdom of Christ." He
shows that so-called "Church Principles "*would, in effect, unchurch
every church on earth,*" owing to the additions and developments since
the days of the Apostles, the changed form of modern Episcopacy,
and the non-retention of certain Apostolic agencies. Bishop Lightfoot points out that *Sacerdotalism* is quite a distinct thing from
Episcopacy, and was not associated with it for a long time subsequent
to the days of the Apostles.

perfect in all its parts, and of exclusively Divine appointment, *answering to the typical "pattern"* given to Moses for the Levitical hierarchy, polity, ceremonies, and sacrifices of the Jewish Church (Heb. viii. 1-5), *is to be found in the New Testament*.

Eminently learned archbishops, bishops, and divines of our Church, *who were also loving, truthful, and candid*, have admitted that, although, in their opinion, *Episcopacy of a moderate and right kind* was a *more complete* polity, yet, that non-Episcopal orders were *perfectly valid and allowable*. So held, for instance, Archbishops Cranmer, Parker, Whitgift, and Usher ; Bishop Cosin, a High Churchman, Bishop Hall, Hooker, and others ; and they acted consistently with such convictions not only in cordial and brotherly relations with the ministers of foreign Protestant churches, but in readiness to commemorate with them the Lord's Supper in their Presbyterian churches. "That any one kind of Government," says Archbishop Whitgift, "is so necessary that . . . . it may not be altered into some other kind thought to be more expedient, I utterly deny. . . . . I find no one certain kind of

Government prescribed or commanded in the Scriptures to the Church of Christ." *

"Mr. Keble himself admits," says Dean Goode, "that nearly up to the time when Hooker wrote, numbers had been admitted to the ministry of the Church in England with no better than Presbyterian ordination."† Dean Goode quotes Archbishop Usher as "towards the close of his life speaking of the foreign Protestant non-Episcopal Churches," and saying, "'I do love and honour [them] as true members of the Church universal,' and 'I do profess that with like affection I should receive the blessed sacrament at the hands of the Danish ministers, if I were in Holland, as I should do at the hands of the French ministers, if I were in Charentone.'" ‡

But the chief hostility to Bishop Jewel was,

---

* Strype's "Whitgift" 406, 408, or Oxf. ed., 159, 173, quoted in Dean Goode's pamphlet, "Brotherly Communion with the Foreign Protestant Churches," p. 11. (Hatchard, 1859.)

† Preface to "Hooker," p. lxxvi. Goode, p. 17.

‡ "Judgment of the late Archbishop of Armagh," &c., by N. Bernard, (Lond., 1657, 8vo.), pp. 123-127. Goode, p. 23. Certain of our bishops and clergy in these days appear to have forgotten, and others, perhaps from "economical" withholding of the truth, have not frankly confessed that the 55th Canon of the Church of England directs her clergy to pray for the Presbyterian Church in Scotland, *as a branch of the Catholic Church.*

no doubt, on account of his refutation of *Sacer-dotalism*, and of his famous challenge to the Roman Catholic divines, which is as follows :—

" In the year 1560, on the Sunday before Easter, Bishop Jewel preached at Paul's Cross his famous sermon upon 1 Cor. xi. 23. This sermon gave a fatal blow to the Popish religion here in England, which was become very odious to all men, by reason of the barbarous cruelty used by those of that persuasion in the reign of Queen Mary ; but the challenge which he then made, and afterwards several times and in several places repeated, was the most stinging part of this sermon, and, therefore, I will insert this famous piece at large."

If any learned man of our adversaries (said he), or all learned men that be alive, be able to bring one sufficient sentence out of any old Catholic doctor, or father, or general council, or holy Scripture, or any one example in the Primitive Church, whereby it may clearly and plainly be proved during the first six hundred years :—

1. That there was at any time any private masses in the world.

2. Or, that there was then any Communion

ministered unto the people under one kind.
[The Roman Catholic Church denies the cup to
the laity.]

3. Or, that the people had their Common
Prayer in a strange tongue that the people
understand not.

4. Or, that the Bishop of. Rome was then
called a universal bishop, or the head of the
Universal Church.

5. Or, that the people were then taught to
believe that Christ's body is really, substantially, corporally, carnally, or naturally, in the
Sacrament.

6. Or, that His body is, or may be, in a
thousand places or more at one time.

7. Or, that the priest did then hold up the
Sacrament over his head.

8. Or, that the people did then fall down and
worship it with godly honour.

9. Or, that the Sacrament was then, or ought
to be, hanged up under a canopy.

10. Or, that in the Sacrament, after the words
of consecration, there remained only the accidents and shows without the substance of bread
and wine.

11. Or, that then the priest divided the

Sacraments into three parts, and afterwards received himself alone.

12. Or, that whosoever had said the Sacrament is a figure, a pledge, a token, or a remembrance of Christ's body, had, therefore, been
adjudged for a heretic.

13. Or, that it was lawful then to have thirty
twenty, fifteen, ten, or five masses said in the
same church in one day.

14. Or, that images were then set up in the
churches, to the intent that people might worship them.

15. Or, that the lay people were then forbidden to read the Word of God in their own
tongues.

16. Or, that it was then lawful for the priest
to pronounce the words of consecration closely,
or in private to himself.

17. Or, that the priest had then authority to
offer up Christ unto the Father.

18. Or, to communicate and receive the
Sacrament for another as they do.

19. Or, to apply the virtue of Christ's death
and passion to any man by means of the mass.

20. Or, that it was then thought a sound
doctrine to teach the people that mass *ex opere*

operato (that is, even for that it is said and done) is able to remove any part of our sin.

21. Or, that any Christian man called the Sacrament of the Lord " his God."

22. Or, that the people were then taught to believe that the body of Christ remaineth in the Sacrament as long as the accidents of bread and wine remain there without corruption.

23. Or, that a mouse or any other beast or worm may eat the body of Christ (for so some of our adversaries have said and taught).

24. Or, that when Christ said *Hoc est corpus Meum* [*i.e.*, this is My body], the word *Hoc* pointed not to the bread, but to an *individuum vagum*, as some of them say.

25. Or, that the accidents, or forms, or shows of bread and wine be the Sacraments of Christ's body and blood, and not rather the very bread and wine itself.

26. Or, that the Sacrament is a sign or token of the body of Christ that lieth hidden underneath it.

27. Or, that ignorance is the mother, and cause of true devotion. The conclusion is, that I shall then be content to yield and subscribe.

" This challenge, says the learned Dr. Heylyn,

" being thus published in so great an auditory, startled the English Papists both at home and abroad."

" This challenge has now been before the world for three hundred years, and no Roman Catholic divine has ever taken it up."—*Catholic Layman*, vol. v. p. 97.*

The Bishop substantiates the whole of those points in his Defence of his famous Apology. All the essential features of Romanism and Ritualism are answered in his writings, which with their vast historical and theological riches, their keen logic, their remarkable lucidity, and their consecrated wit, will be found by thoughtful laymen a most bracing as well as instructive study. His treatise on the Holy Scriptures is a most precious gem, deserving the widest circulation.

6. " *Puritan*," in Ritualistic interpretations, often means Evangelical clergymen and laymen, *who faithfully teach, and consistently carry out* in their *chancels*, as well as from their *pulpits*, in their hymn books, and otherwise, Scriptural and Protestant principles and practices. In Lon-

---

* Published by the *Protestant Alliance*, 9, Strand, London, W.C. Price 1s. per 100, post free.

don, and in provincial newspapers, more or less
under Romish or Ritualistic influences, it is
either ignorantly or spitefully used as a term
of reproach, at which Christ's faithful servants
may good-naturedly and forgivingly smile, in the
spirit of New Testament ethics, such as those in
1 Cor. xiii., and Rom. xii.*

PROTESTANTISM is fairly represented, for all
practical purposes, in the Articles and Confessions of Faith of the various Churches, Episcopal
and non-Episcopal.† They will be found to
agree wonderfully in the fundamental doctrines
of the Christian religion, and substantially to
exhibit the truth of a saying of the historian,
Dr. Merle D'Aubigné, that " Unity amidst
diversity, and variety in unity, such is the law
of nature, such should be the law of the
Church."

True, alas ! it is, that, owing to the natural
depravity of the human heart, and to the ceaseless and humbling workings within all of us of

---

* For a most interesting and impartial account of the *historical*
Puritans, see the Rev. J. B. Marsden's two volumes on "The Early
Puritans" and "The Later Puritans."

† See "Harmony of the Protestant Confessions," edited by Rev.
Peter Hall, M.A. (John F. Shaw, 1842.) Also, "Essays on Christian
Union," with Introduction by Dr. Merle D'Aubigné (1857), and
other publications initiated by the *Evangelical Alliance.*

that "old man," or "law in our members"
(Rom. vii.), "warring against" the teaching and
example of Christ, and more or less outraging
Bible principles, Protestant Churches, whether
Episcopal or non-Episcopal, have manifested
within themselves and towards other Churches
scandalous denominational selfishness, jealousy,
self-exaltation, ambition, and "love of pre-
eminence." Even the Apostles were tempted by
the evil one to quarrel amongst themselves as
to who "should be the greatest."* This occurred,
too, after their partaking of the heart affecting
Lord's Supper. † Such sinful conduct has by no
means been discontinued. Do we not still
witness the most glaring disobedience to such
plain and practical precepts as these, addressed
by our Lord and Master to His truly converted
and believing people :—"If ye love Me, keep My
commandments. . . . . If a man love Me, he will
keep My words. . . . . He that loveth Me not,
keepeth not My sayings."‡ "This is My
commandment, That ye love one another, as I
have loved you." § "He that saith, I know
[Jesus Christ] and keepeth not His command-

---

* Mark ix. 32-42. † Luke xxii. 14-27. ‡ John xiv. 15, 23.
§ John xv. 12.

ments, is a liar, and the truth is not him."*
"We know that we have passed from death
unto life, because we love the brethren. . . . .
Let us not love in word, neither in tongue ; but
in deed and in truth."† "Be kindly affectioned
one to another with brotherly love, in honour
preferring one another."‡ "Love worketh no
ill to his neighbour : therefore love is the
fulfilling of the law."§ "Let all bitterness, and
wrath, and anger, and clamour, and evil speaking, be put away from you, with all malice : and
be ye kind to one another, tender-hearted,
forgiving one another, even as God for Christ's
sake hath forgiven you."¶ "Look not every man
on his own things, but every man also on the
things of others. Let this mind be in you,
which was also in Christ Jesus."‖

Certainly, transgressions against such obligatory teaching is most reprehensible. But, on
the other hand, does Romanism appear in a
more heavenly aspect ? Has that spiritual
Babylon—that woman " sitting on the seven
mountains," urging on the horrible tortures
and murders of the INQUISITION, and " drunken

---

* John ii. 4.   † 1 John iii. 14, 18.   Rom. xii. 10.   § Rom. xiii. 10.
¶ Ephes. iv. 31, 32.   ‖ Phil. ii. 3-5.

with the blood of the saints, and with the blood
of the martyrs of Jesus "*—has she any good
grounds for boasting of her higher regard for
the teaching of the Word of God? If not,
how, with her boasted superiority, is it so?
Protestants are fatally weakened by their
internal and external dissensions; on the other
hand, although, as a fact, the dissensions within the Church of Rome have been quite equal to
those in Protestant Churches,† yet, from her iron
discipline, the tremendous spiritual blessings
and terrors that she claims and is believed by
her priest-led followers by Divine right to
exercise, and the manifold sensuous, theatrical,
material, and worldly agencies at her disposal,
on what a vantage ground does she tower!

Yet, in reality, as Napoleon said that whereas
his power and his empire rested on FORCE,
Christ's kingdom was governed by LOVE, and
that multitudes of believers in Him were ready
out of grateful love to suffer and to die for Him;
so is it as regards the Church of Rome. Hers
is A RELIGION OF FEAR AND OF DOUBT

---

* Rev. xvii. 1-9.

† See "The Variations of Popery," by Rev. Samuel Edgar (2nd ed.,
Seeley, 1838).

THROUGHOUT LIFE. Hidden is the light of the glorious Gospel of a free and full pardon of all sin, through the righteousness and the one all-atoning Sacrifice of Christ on Calvary's cross, as the loving Substitute for his Bride (Ephes. v. 25-32), and for "the sins of the whole world;" the sweet peace of mind, the happy conscience, the removal of fear in death wrought in Christ's freely chosen followers, regenerated by the Holy Spirit as the Divine agent, through God's written Word as His instrument;* the comforting, cheering, and upholding promises of His effectual help under all our sorrows, trials, and conflicts with the world, the flesh, and the devil, and the certainty that, sooner or later, He will perfectly purify us, thoroughly educate us for heaven, and change us into a glorious likeness to Christ. Such, and other precious Bible truths, are hidden from our poor Roman Catholic brethren, for whom, if, through the unmerited grace of God, we are safe in Christ, we ought to feel the tenderest pity and most practical sympathy, as well as for Ritualists and all other "neighbours" similarly circumstanced.

---

* Ephes. vi. 13-18; 2 Thess. ii. 13-17; James i. 16, 17; 1 Peter i. 18-25.

No Roman Catholic, no Ritualist is capable of grateful love to Christ, according to their religion, which is the very opposite to the Christian faith of the Bible. They could not, with deep penitential gratitude, use the glowing language of the Apostle Paul, and say, " I have been crucified with Christ: yet I live ; *and yet* no longer I, but Christ liveth in me : and that *life* which I now live in the flesh I live in faith, *the faith* which is in the Son of God, who loved me, and gave Himself up for me."* Nor could those poor doubting and disbelieving souls respond to the happy certainty of faith, of which the Apostle John writes when he says, " Beloved, now are we the sons of God, and it doth not yet appear what we shall be : but we know that, when He shall appear, we shall be like Him ; for we shall see Him as He is. And every man that hath this hope in Him purifieth himself even as He is pure."†

Nor can unhappy, doubting, and disbelieving souls experience true love and gratitude towards Christ, on account of believing that " God for

---

* Gal. ii. 20, R.V.

† 1 John iii. 1-3. The same Apostle further says, " We know that we have passed from death unto life, because we love the brethren " (v. 14).

Christ's sake hath forgiven them " (Ephes.
iv. 32)—that, through the precious blood-shed-
ing of His life, freely laid down as their all-
atoning sacrifice, their "sins are forgiven them
for His name's sake," justly, righteously, and
holily (1 John i. 7, ii. 12; Rom. iii. 19-27;
2 Cor. v. 14-21, vi. 1), and that they, NOW,
through faith in Christ, "have everlasting
life, and shall not come into condemnation, but are passed from death unto life "
(John v. 24; Rom. v. 24, iii. 14-18),
and that Christ, *by His Spirit and
through the written Word* in connection with
various means of grace, and not through Sacraments only nor chiefly, is " purifying them unto
Himself," and making them more and more
holy, especially by sanctified afflictions (Titus
ii. 13-15; Heb. xii. 1-14), and that God is making " *all* things work together for their good,"
until He consummates their happiness in
heaven.

Unless, through grace, they are taught to
comprehend the condition of " the natural man "
(1 Cor. ii. 9-15), and " carnal mind " which is
" enmity with God " (Rom. viii. 5-9; Ephes. ii.
1-10), how can they be filled with humble,

penitential, yet rejoicing gratitude for their having, through unmerited grace, been " chosen in Christ before the foundation of the world " ? (Eph. i. 1-7). How can they "love much because much is forgiven " ? (Luke viii. 40-50) ; or how, in reading those deeply impressive words of our blessed Lord and Master, " No man can come unto Me, except the Father which hath sent Me draw him : and I will raise him up at the last day," and " him that cometh unto Me, I will in no wise cast out " (John vi. 37, 44, 45)—how can they have their hearts rightly affected by *a self-application* of the assuring and inspiriting declaration, " I have loved thee with an everlasting love ; therefore with lovingkindness have I drawn thee" (Jer. xxxi. 3); or sympathize rightly in the grateful feelings of the converted Apostle, once " a persecutor and a blasphemer," but *then* filled with burning love and adoring praise of " the Son of God," who, he says, " loved *me*, and gave Himself for *me* " ? How can they rightly sing :—

" Jesus sought me when a stranger,
 Wandering from the fold of God,
 He, to save my soul from danger,
 Interposed His precious blood " ?

F 2

Or,

> " I was a wandering sheep,
> I did not love the fold,
> I did not love my Shepherd's voice,
> I would not be controlled " ?

Or how honour Christ by believing the precious
promise, " I will in no wise fail thee ; neither
will I in any wise forsake thee " so that, with
good courage, we may be able gladly to say,
" The Lord is my helper ; I will not fear : what
shall man do unto me ? (Heb. xiii. 5-6, R.V.). Or
how, with the Apostle, help to cheer on fellow-
believers amidst " fears within and fightings
without," by expressing " confidence of this very
thing, that he which began a good work in
[them] will perfect it until the day of Jesus
Christ" ? (Phil. i. 5-6, R.V.). Or, how duly
appreciate the Scriptural truths in the Seventeenth Article of the Church of England, or join
experimentally and heartily in the grand
" general thanksgiving " in the Liturgy ?

Oh, how sweet, how precious beyond words
to express, is a personal experience, the work
of the Spirit, such as is thus described by Dr.
SIBBES, " the silver-tongued " Puritan divine,
in his " Divine Meditations and Contempla-

tions "! "The love of Christ manifested to
me," he observes, " and my love to Christ,
quickened by the Spirit, excite a holy
admiration in my soul : it considers what
wonderful love is in Christ; and the Spirit
witnesses that this love of Christ is set
upon the soul : from hence it begins to argue
and admire ; 'Lord, wherefore wilt Thou show
Thyself to me, and not to the world.? What is
the reason Thou so lovest me more than others ? '
The soul with God on the mount is turned from
earthly things, then it sees nothing but love and
mercy, and adores. Such grace constrains us to
do all things out of pure love to God and good
will towards men."

But are not God's truly adopted children in
Christ, on their way to His presence and to
heaven, subject, at times, to sinful doubts and
fears of the fulfilment to *them* of a covenant-
keeping God and Father's faithful promises—
not in *them,* and not for *their* righteousness, but
"*in* CHRIST" and because of *His* righteousness ?
Alas ! yes. Believers may have humbling,
penitential convictions, and harassing apprehensions, and sore woes that we may " procure
unto ourselves" by *exceptional* sins and incon-

sistencies (Jer. ii. 17-19 ; 1 John ii. 1-6), at
variance with a true child of God's *habitual*
state, and by loving and pitiful "rebukes" and
" chastenings" for which (Rev. iii. 15-19) Christ
may appear to us to have forsaken us. But all
the while, is He not promoting and deepening
in His "little ones who believe in Him" humility
meekness, gentleness, patience, purity, compassion for, and sympathy with, struggling brethren
in Christ, and fellow-sinners generally, and more
devoted exertion on behalf of the Jews and the
heathen millions—in other words, furthering in
us all the lovely features of heavenly love
(1 Cor. xiii.), and all that is comprised in that
wonderful word "Holiness"? Beyond all that
experience of why "for a small moment [our
God] has forsaken us," but, *in due time,*
"with great mercies will gather us" (Isa.
liv. 1-8)—are not even true believers liable to
be tempted to sin, by practically and injuriously
forgetting that vile as are *all* sins, yet that the
chiefest and most prolific sin is said to be
"because [men] *believe not on* CHRIST"
(John xvi. 1-3), and that it is most sinful in us
to " receive the witness of men," in believing
each other's word, or expecting such honour

from one another, whereas "the witness of God
is greater," and that "he that believeth not
God hath made Him a liar; because he
believeth not the record that God gave of His
Son. And this is the record, that God has
given to us eternal life, and this life is in His
Son," so that "we may know that we have
eternal life, that we may believe on the name
of the Son of God."—"He that hath the Son
hath life, and he that hath not the Son of God
hath not life"? (1 John v. 9-13 ; John v. 39-47).

The Apostle Paul writes, "Now he which
stablisheth us with you in Christ, and hath
anointed us, is God; who hath also sealed us,
and given the earnest of the Spirit in our
hearts" (2 Cor. i. 21, 22).

St. John writes, "He that keepeth His
commandments dwelleth in Him, and He in him.
And hereby we know that He abideth in
us, by the Spirit which He hath given us"
(1 John iii. 24).

If we *know* that "the things of the Spirit of
God" are *not* "foolishness unto us," as they
are to the "natural" or unconverted and un-
saved man, who "*cannot* know them" (1 Cor.
ii. 13, 14) ; and, if we *know* that we are *not* in

a state of " enmity against God," as the " carnally minded " are (Rom. viii. 5-6), but that we
long to love God in Christ more, and to serve
Him better—is it not evident that we *cannot* be
" dead in trespasses and sins," but have been
"quickened" by the Holy Spirit? (Ephes. ii.
1-10). If so, ought we not, with humble, grateful hearts, to "joy in God through our Lord
Jesus Christ, through whom we have now
received the atonement"? (Rom. v. 1-11).

Some of the Tractarian leaders actually advo-
cated *reserve* in proclaiming the full Gospel of
Christ. In his volume on the Arians, Mr.
Newman thus expresses their views on " public
preaching " :—"There are," he says, " very many
sincere Christians of the present day who consider that the evangelical doctrines are the
appointed instruments of conversion, and, as
such, exclusively attended with the Divine
blessing." That view he endeavours with remarkable sophistry to refute, using some of the
Fathers, who, according to his representation
(which, however, needs careful verification from
the writings of Clement and Tertullian), observed an *alleged* " apostolical rule " for a
" cautious distribution of sacred truth." Accord-

ing to the statement of Mr. Newman, " The
Fathers *considered that they had the pattern as
well as the recommendation of this procedure in
Scripture itself.*" *
"Surely," says Mr. Newman, " the sacred
volume was not intended, and is not adapted to
teach us our creed,† however certain it is when

---

* Unhappily, the quotations from the Fathers, and representations
of the views set forth in their writings by Tractarian writers, cannot be trusted. For instance, Dr. PUSEY published a volume purport-
ing to be an accurate compilation from the works of the Fathers, and,
according to which, those ancient writers upheld the Romanist and
Tractarian doctrine of what is averred to be *the* " real presence " of our
Lord's body and blood, effected by the potent use of the words, " this
is My body " in the Lord's Supper. Dr. Pusey, in an evil hour for him,
challenged contradiction. The Rev. Dr. John Harrison, in his learned
and accurate "Answer to Dr. Pusey's Challenge"—a work not refuted by
Romanists or Ritualists —*supplied scores of the contexts* left out by Dr.
Pusey, and proved that the latter had disingenuously *misrepresented*
the teaching of the Fathers *in toto.*

See also Dean Goode's work on the Eucharist, and his "Divine Rule
of Faith and Practice." .

† The Word of God " not intended, and adapted to teach us our
creed"! Is that, or is it not, blasphemy against its Divine Author?
" When Rome," said Bishop Christopher Wordsworth, on Rev.
xvii. 3, " withholds the HOLY SCRIPTURES from her people (and she has
never printed at Rome a single copy of the Old Testament in its
original language), and when she bestows honour on those who revile
Scripture, calling it imperfect, ambiguous, a mute Judge [like Cardinal
Newman], a leaden Rule," and by other opprobrious names,‡ is she
not guilty of blasphemy against the Divine Author of Scripture ? "

What sort of sermons could be expected of Mr. Newman, wonderful

---

‡ See some of them cited by Bishop Andrewes, Adv. Bellarmine,
cap. xi. pp. 259, 260, and Casaubon, in Exerc. Baron, i. xxxiii. See
also Letter iv. of Sequel of Letters to M. Goudon, " Union with
Rome," &c., 8th ed., p. 46.

it has once been taught us, and in spite of individual producible exceptions to the general rule. From the very first that rule has been, as a matter of fact, for the Church to teach the truth, and then appeal to Scripture in vindication of its own teaching."

Yes! "CHURCH TEACHING" set above "BIBLE TRUTH," and made to *transform its true meaning*, just as the word "church," which also means "an assembly" or "a congregation," and not one only, is transformed so as to signify *the* MINISTERS of *the* Christian Church, or, as Ritualists prefer expressing it, her "sacrificing priests."

But how, it may be asked, are we simple folk to know *for certain* what *is* "the Church"? Are we to take it on the assertion of the "priests," and then be cajoled or *disciplined* into looking through *their* spectacles for Scripture proof? Can "the Church," or, indeed, what is *not* "the Church," be surely known apart from the Holy Bible itself?

---

master of the English language as he was, on such Scriptures as Ps. xix., cxix., or on the following passage:—"All Scripture is given by inspiration of God, and is profitable for doctrine, for reproof, for correction, for instruction in righteousness: that the man of God may be perfect, thoroughly furnished unto all good works"? (2 Tim. iii. 16, 17).

IMPLICIT OBEDIENCE to the CHURCH is a primary law in the anti-Christian Church of Rome. It is declared to be *holy* obedience, and is most effectual in furthering the deceptions, the misrepresentations, the cruelties, the iniquities, and the tyranny of priests, abbesses, mothers of sisterhoods, and other executive personages.

A striking illustration of Rome's unchanged and unchangeable *fundamental* principles of cruelty, terrorism, assassination, and murder, according to her CANON LAW, is given in Mr. Gladstone's comparison between Cardinal Newman and one of Rome's most learned theologians and most eminent men, Dr. Döllinger. I quote from an Article in *Evangelical Christendom*, for October, 1890, citing Mr. Gladstone's article in the *Speaker*, August 30th.

Mr. Gladstone remarks that "the construction of Döllinger's mind was simple, that of Newman's complex." Of that truth some illustrations have been given in these pages. The Cardinal's mind was, indeed, "complex," and like unto the "*Maze*" or labyrinth of the Church of Rome, which so enlightened Hooker, and which is in such startling contrast with "the simplicity that is in Christ" (2 Cor. xi. 1-3, 13-15).

Well may we exclaim with our Christian poet, Cowper :—

> "Oh, how unlike the complex arts of man,
> Is heaven's easy, unencumbered plan !"

Dr. Döllinger's "honesty of character," as sketched by Mr. Gladstone, would not allow him to accept the dogma of the Pope's personal infallibility, in the light of ecclesiastical history, nor even in that of the Church of Rome herself. He invincibly felt, says Mr. Gladstone, that "strong conviction of a matter of fact, founded on scores of years spent in the special study of it, makes it difficult to contradict upon oath." That "difficulty of contradicting upon oath" the real facts of history, or of the Church of Rome's real teaching, was not felt by the Roman Catholic bishops in facilitating the adoption of the Roman Catholic Emancipation Bill to our cost.*

---

* On the extraordinary conduct of the Roman Catholic bishops in wickedly leading our politicians and statesmen astray, see full proof in "The Nullity of the Government of Queen Victoria in Ireland, and an Exhibition of the Laws of the Papacy," by the Rev. Robert J. McGhee, A.M. (2nd ed., Seeley, 1841).

Mr. McGhee proves that, whilst denied in the most solemn manner by the Roman Catholic bishops, in reality "the most infamous, the

Mr. Gladstone, observes the writer in *Evangelical Christendom*, "ends this interesting article by pointing out the danger from assassination to which [Dr. Döllinger's] honesty exposed him, quoting the Canon Law, which says, ' We do not count them to be homicides to whom it may have happened, through their burning zeal for Mother Church against the excommunicated, to put any of these to death.' "

Is it not remarkable that " the APOSTASY " within the professing Churches of what is known as " Christendom " is said to be energized by Satan, " the prince of this world," usurping supreme power over the whole earth (2 Thess.

most treasonable, the most persecuting, the most atrocious Bulls of the Popes were kept ready for use at a favourable opportunity. One of them, *the Third Canon of the Fourth Lateran Council*, is a law for the deposition of the sovereign being Protestant, and for the universal massacre of Protestants, as it was, when enacted in 1215, for the slaughter of the Albigenses. . . . . It is a law of which the best description is given by a Papal Bishop, Dr. Doyle, when it was his interest to deny it. It is a law, as he says, ' *to upturn the foundations of society, and to drench our streets and our fields in blood*'" (pp. 294, 295). An analysis of the Canon Law has been drawn up by Mr. Charles Hastings Collette, the learned and well-known author of many valuable works on the Church of Rome. In particular, a volume on "The Novelties of Romanism" (published by the Religious Tract Society), replies to Milner's End Controversy, and to the recent work on "Catholic Belief," &c., &c. The analysis of the Canon Law is published by the Protestant Alliance, at the small cost of 2d., with a view to its wide circulation.

ii. 7-10 ; John xiv. 30, xii. 26, 27, xvii. 12), and symbolized by the " son of perdition," or " false apostle" (2 Cor. xi. 1-3, 13-15), and that a chief characteristic of Satan, as given by our God and Saviour, is that, " He was a murderer from the beginning, and abode not in the truth, because there is no truth in him. When he speaketh of a lie, he speaketh of his own : for he is a liar, and the father of it " ? (John viii. 44).

So also the professing Christian apostasy was to be retributively given over to " strong delusion that they should believe a lie " (2 Thess. ii.).

They sincerely and " religiously " believe it, and yet all the while it is " a lie ! "

That enslaving obedience effectually puts out the light of God's holy truth, keeps the laity in ignorance, and, like the careful prohibition even of a friendly, properly conducted, and impartial visitation of convents, under the convenient plea of " unwarrantable intrusion," or of " invading sacred precincts," prevents wronged victims from being righted. In *some* cases—it may, too, possibly be in *many* cases—why may it not be . known to God, though not to the outside world, that the Scripture has been too sadly verified, which says, " Every one that doeth evil hateth

the light, neither cometh to the light, lest his
deeds be reproved. But he that loveth truth
cometh to the light, that his deeds may be
made manifest, that they are wrought in
God "? (John iii. 20, 21).

Mr. Newman evidently felt, as in the case of
his " Tract XC.," that there were serious difficulties in the way of propagating " economy " as
regards withholding the light of Gospel truth
and the facts of history, or of " explaining "
them away.

For, in his characteristic way, he first states
a formidable difficulty thus :—" A more plausible
objection to the existence of this rule of secrecy
in the early Church arises from the circumstance
that the Christian apologies openly mention to
the whole world the sacred tenets which have
been above represented as the peculiar possession
of the confirmed believer."

Now, the *facts* involved in the nature of the
"Christian apologies," Mr. Newman cannot and
does not deny. How does he set about to try
and nullify their force ? Thus :—" But it must
be observed," he says, " that the writers of
these were frequently laymen, and so did not
commit the Church as a body, nor even in its

separate authorities, to formal statement or to theological discussion."*

Now, suppose that those writers were "*lay-men.*" What then? Is not the real question, above all, *this*, namely, did they state *the truth?* Is not the *light* altogether independent of *the candlestick?* Does not the "Father of lights"† freely bestow, in such measure as it may please Him, the light of truth on all the living members of Christ, who, as such, whether clergy or laity, are part of the same "royal priesthood, and holy nation, and peculiar people," formed by the Holy Spirit to "show forth the praises of Him who hath called them out of darkness into His marvellous light"?

Without interfering in any way with or diminishing from the special offices, duties, and privileges of *their brother "priests" and fellow-believers in Christ,*‡ who, in their respective Christian Churches, whether Episcopal or non-Episcopal, have been ordained or "consecrated," whether as bishops, presbyters, pastors, deacons, to minister within their respective churches and chapels; is not Gospel *truth*, or

---

* "Arians," pp. 50-57. † James i. 14-18.
‡ 1 Peter i. 1-10 ; Rev. i. 5-7.

historical *truth*, or any other truth, whether as regards doctrines or facts, of equal value from whomsoever they may instrumentally come? Waiving all other illustrations, does not the inspired Apostle call on the Philippian *laity*, to "be blameless and harmless, the sons of God, without rebuke, in the midst of a crooked and perverse nation, among whom," he adds " ye shine as lights in the world, holding forth the word of life ; * that I may rejoice in the day of Christ, that I have not run in vain, neither laboured in vain." For the loving Apostle desired to " joy, and rejoice with them all "?

Have not learned, wise, and truly great men expressed their readiness, *out of love of truth for truth's sake*, to receive truth by the ministry of a little child? Have not very distinguished persons gladly availed themselves of the *light* down in the Cornish or other mines, though such light came not from refined wax, but from tallow candles, not in golden candlesticks, but stuck into a lamp of clay, or placed in a cleft of the rock?

---

* Phil. ii. 14-16, "Holding forth," that is, as the hand holds a torch. See Scott and Matthew Henry *in loco*.

One chief element of the alleged superiority
of the Roman Catholic Church over all other
Churches is her claim—as baseless as all her
other claims—to her UNITY, offering a splendid
contrast to the inferior condition of Protestants,
divided as they are.   Well, they *are* living *in
separate outward folds or forms of Church
Government*.   Like the variations in nature, of
which our Christian poet Cowper so beautifully
says, " It is the name for *an effect*, whose *cause*
is God," Protestant Churches have variety as
their characteristic.   They have not *uniformity*.

Now, all the Churches on earth are on a level
in one essential and very suggestive feature.
They have "one and all" within them both
" tares " and " wheat."   The " tares " may not
be all of one kind.   For, of course, the Church of
England, inheriting Cathedrals, a hierarchy, and
other features, is more open to the Ritualistic
theatrical dresses, pomp, and sensuousness, and
to architectural Popery than non-Episcopal
Churches.   But the latter have their deplorable
" *down grades* " in some heretical form or other,
as, for instance, the denial of the atonement of
Christ, and of eternal punishment, assaults on the
inspiration and authority of God's Word, and

other pernicious errors. So will it be until our
Lord and Saviour comes again the second time.*
Even the Church of Rome, with all her stupend-
ous claims to be regarded as the Church of all
Churches on earth, and to possess so immense a
monopoly of grace over Protestants, does not
deny that Scripture truth. She has *good*
" Catholics," [which is by no means the same
thing as good *Christians* in the Bible sense]
who, poor souls ! have to go into a purgatory,†
because on earth they were not thoroughly
cleansed through the Gospel that " the blood
of Jesus Christ cleanseth from ALL sin." The
Church of Rome teaches that lucrative doctrine,
in defiance of the declarations of Holy Scripture,

---

* Matt. xiii. 24-30.

† It has been cogently asked, If there is such a place as purgatory
resembling the locality in heathen mythology, and if the priests of the
Church of Rome are really able by Masses, or otherwise, to get poor
souls out of their sufferings, why, as "loving their neighbour as
they love themselves," do they not *get them out at once?* and that,
moreover, generously, "without money and without price" (Isa. lv.
1-9), and as impelled by the heart-affecting appeal of the Apostle
Peter to practical morality and pity when he says, "Forasmuch as ye
know that ye were not redeemed with corruptible things, as silver and
gold, from your vain conversation *received* by tradition from your
fathers, but with the precious blood of Christ, as of a lamb without
blemish and without spot " (1 Peter i. 15-21).

Is it not remarkable that the character given in prophecy to spiritual
Babylon includes the charge of her making "merchandise " out of the
souls of men"? (Rev. xviii. 4-13).

G 2

that the everlasting condition of every one of us is irrevocably sealed at the moment of death, and that accordingly no hope whatever is held out of any future salvation for any one who dies unfortunate, unbelieving, and impenitent.*

The Church of England, also, too many of whose bishops and clergy teach the pernicious doctrine of *Baptismal Regeneration, irrespective of faith and repentance preceding baptism,* although the Catechism declares the absolute necessity "for persons ["infants" included] *to be* baptized," that they shall possess " repentance whereby they forsake sin, and faith whereby they steadfastly believe the promises of God," our Church, in one of her Articles, declares that " in the visible Church, the evil be ever mingled with the good." Is it not so in the case of the Lord's Supper ? †

But if Protestants have not uniformity, yet all true members of Christ within their Churches, all who are not " tares " but " wheat," *neces-sarily,* through the power of the Holy Spirit, and the promises in and by Christ, possess true

---

* Eccles. viii. 10-13, ix. 5, 6, 10 ; Ps. vi. 5, lxxxviii. 10 ; Ps. xxxviii. 18, 19 ; John iii. 36 ; Matt. xxv. 31-46 ; Gal. vii. 7, 8 ; John viii. 21-24 ; Rev. xx. 11-15, xxii. 11-12.

† Matt. vii. 21-23 ; Luke xiii. 24-27 ; 1 Cor. xi. 27-30.

UNITY, although, to the shame of too many amongst them, they do not openly acknowledge that unity in their one Head before "the world" to His glory, to the glory of the Holy Spirit's work within all of them, and to their mutual fellowship and rejoicing together as elect members of the royal family of heaven, who are to dwell together and serve and praise our one Lord and Saviour up there for ever and ever.

But what is the boasted UNITY of the Church of Rome, with its *Uniformity of the Grave?* That boasted unity is a spurious unity, and her charge of SCHISM recoils with an overwhelming crash on her own head. This is powerfully shown, amongst other learned writers, by Bishop Christopher Wordsworth, as we shall presently see.

We must distinguish carefully between the schism against which we are especially warned in HOLY SCRIPTURE, which means *separation from Christ and Gospel truth,* and what is re- garded as schism in human and ecclesiastical

---

* Compare John iii. 16, 17, 18, 36, xv. 1-11, vi. 64-71 ; 1 John iv. 1-6 ; 2 John 7-11 ; Gal. i. 6-9, ii. 3-16 ; Heb. v. 1-9 ; 1 Tim. iv. 1-5 ; 1 Peter ii. 1-3 ; Matt. vii. 15-23.

language, and which signifies *separation from some visible Church.* The Church of Rome, indeed, claims to be not only a true Christian Church, which, in the light of the Bible and of history, is more than can be granted, but she even claims to be *the Mistress of all Churches,* and declares that separation from *her* is soul-destroying.

Now, up to the time of the Council of Trent, the Episcopal Churches were, according to the orthodox view, mutually eligible to unity and inter-communion, by virtue of their giving their assent and consent to the three Creeds, and more particularly to the Nicene Creed. No particular Church was allowed to put forth any additional articles of belief, as terms of communion, and much less as necessary to salvation. For ecclesiastical schism is caused in two ways : namely, by unjustifiable and needless separation from a visible professing Christian Church, whose fundamental terms of communion are Scriptural; or, secondly, by the enforcement by any Church of novel and unorthodox terms of communion, *rendering her the authoress of schism,* and communion with her to be *schism from Episcopal* CHRISTENDOM, which, in the eyes of many sincere and conscientious High Churchmen, is regarded as equivalent to separation from Christ and salvation. Now, at the Council of Trent, the Creed of Pope Pius IV., with twelve new articles, was adopted by the Roman Catholic Church, and enforced as terms of communion, thus superseding and setting at naught the three Creeds of Christendom, and schismatically breaking the continuity of Episcopal communion previously maintained.

On Unity and Schism connected with the Church of Rome the late Bishop of Lincoln, Dr. Christopher Wordsworth, thus writes :—

" The Fathers *could* not *foresee* that, in the sixteenth century after Christ, the Church of Rome, at the Council of Trent, would add Twelve Articles to the Nicene Creed, and that she would impose those articles on all men, as terms of communion, and as necessary to salvation. The Fathers could not foresee that in the nineteenth century after Christ the Church of Rome would add another new article to ' *the faith once delivered to the Saints,*'* by decreeing that the Blessed Virgin Mary was exempt from

---

* Jude 3.

original sin.* They would have recoiled from such a notion as incredible. Indeed, one of our strongest objections to the Church of Rome is, that she enforces doctrines which the ancient *Fathers never knew*, and which (as the Romish advocates of the *Doctrine of Development* allow) she herself did not explicitly profess for many centuries. And, *if* she *had held* these doctrines in the days of the ancient Fathers, then our argument against the *novelty* of these doctrines would fall to the ground.

*   *   *   *   *

"It is not the *main* end and aim of *Prophecy* to warn men now against *Infidelity*, any more than it was formerly against *Paganism*. The power described by St. Paul and St. John in the Apocalypse is expressly called a *Mystery*. But *Infidelity* proclaims itself: *it* is *no* 'mystery.' And Christ has pronounced His sentence, once for all, against Unbelief: '*He that believeth and is baptized shall be saved; but he that believeth not*

---

* As was done on Dec. 8, 1854, when the Church of Rome made "the Immaculate Conception" to be an article of Faith. [In addition to that new article of Faith must be added the crowning blasphemy of the personal infallibility of the Pope, not only raising the official utterances of the Pope to a level with the written Word of God, but in practical effects superseding it.] The addition within brackets is not the Bishop's, whose book was published before that crowning blasphemy was perpetrated.

shall be damned.'* No subsequent voice could add force or clearness to this Divine Verdict.

"But it *is* the legitimate aim and end of Christian Prophecy to warn the world against the insidious designs and mysterious workings of deadly error, masked in the garb of Religion ; for Satan is never so much to be feared as when he is ' *transformed into an angel of light.'†*

"And even *because* Infidelity *is* to be dreaded, this warning against *corrupt Religion* was necessary to be given ; for the state of those who use Religion as a cloak for sin and error is worse than that of Heathens.‡ Superstition is the most prolific source of Atheism. When a People see Religion allying itself with imposture, they soon regard Religion as a fraud. Thus Superstition drives them into Unbelief. This, as the Author of this Essay knows too well from personal observation, is the danger of Italy and France at this time.§

---

* Mark ix. 16.   † 2 Cor. xi. 14.

‡ Hooker, Sermon v. 9 : "*Mockers* (Jude 18) are they that use Religion as a cloak ; who kiss Christ with Judas, and betray Him with Judas. . . . who use truth to subvert truth, yea Scriptures themselves to disprove Scripture. . . . Surely the condition of these men is more lamentable than is the condition of Pagans and Turks."

§ In the present day, all will do well to ponder the words of our great English divine, Bp. Bull. Speaking of certain Romish corrup-

"Looking, then, at the declarations of Scripture concerning Infidelity, and at the two ends of Christian Prophecy, and at the perils of the world from Infidelity, and at the language and spirit of these Apocalyptic prophecies, we see reason to believe, *even* on *this* account, that the form of Antichristianism contemplated by them is *not* a *heathen*, or *infidel*, but a *religious* one.

"9. Many admirable works have been composed by our own divines in vindication of the Church of England from the charge of Schism, preferred against her by Romish Controversialists, on the ground of her conduct at the Reformation, when she cleared herself from Romish errors, novelties, and corruptions.

"It has been shown in those Vindications that it is the bounden duty of all Churches to avoid strife, and to *seek peace, and ensue it.* But it was also demonstrated, no less clearly, that Unity in *error* is *not true* Unity, but is rather to be called a conspiracy against the God of Unity and Truth.

tions, especially in the worship of the Blessed Virgin, ho says, "Wise men have thought that tho authors of these romances in religion were no better than the tools of Satan, used by him to expose the Christian religion, and thereby to introduce *Atheism*."—Bp. Bull, Serm. iv. vol. i. p. 106, ed. Oxf. 1827.

"Doubtless there is a Unity, when everything in Nature is wrapped in the gloom of Night, and bound with the chains of Sleep. Doubtless there is a Unity, when the Earth is congealed by frost, and mantled in a robe of snow. Doubtless there is a Unity, when the human voice is still, the hand motionless, the breath suspended, and the human frame is locked in the iron grasp of Death. And doubtless there is a Unity, when men surrender their Reason, and sacrifice their Liberty, and stifle their Conscience, and seal up Scripture, and deliver themselves captives, bound hand and foot, to the dominion of the Church of Rome. But this is not the Unity of vigilance and light ; it is the Unity of sleep and gloom. It is not the Unity of warmth and life ; it is the Unity of cold and death. It is not true Unity, for it is not UNITY in the TRUTH.

"Therefore, since it has been proved by Appeals to Reason, to Scripture, and to Antiquity, that the Church of Rome has built *hay and stubble on the one foundation laid by Christ ;** that she has added to the faith many errors and corruptions which mar and vitiate it ;

---

* 1 Cor. iii. 12.

and since, as the Holy Spirit teaches us in the
Apocalypse, it is the duty of every Church
which has fallen into error *to repent;** and since
Jesus Christ Himself, our Great High Priest—
*who walketh in the midst of the Golden Candle-
sticks*—declares, that when a Church has *left her
first love*, He will *remove her Candlestick out
of its place, except she repent,†* and *strengthen
the things which remain, that are ready to die ;‡*
and since the corruptions of *one* Church afford
no palliation or excuse for those of *another ;* for,
as the Prophet says, *though Israel play the harlot, let not Judah sin ;§* and as Christ Himself
teaches, though the Church of Sardis be *dead,* ||
and Laodicea be *neither hot nor cold,*¶ yet their
sister Ephesus must *remember whence she has
fallen, and do her first works,*** and Pergamos
must *repent,* or He *will come quickly, and fight
against her with the sword of His mouth*††—
therefore, we say, it was justly concluded by our
divines, that no desire of Unity on our part, nor
reluctance on the part of Rome to cast off her
errors, could exempt England from the duty of
Reformation ; and if Rome, instead of *removing*

---

* Rev. iii. 3.   † Rev. ii. 5.   ‡ Rev. iii. 2.   § Hos. iv. 15.
|| Rev. iii. 1.   ¶ Rev. iii. 15.   ** Rev. ii. 5.   †† Rev. ii. 16.

her corruptions, refused to communicate with England, unless England consented to communicate with Rome in those corruptions, then no love of Unity could justify England in compliance with this requisition of Rome; for Unity in error is not Christian Unity; but, by imposing the necessity of erring as a term of Union, Rome became guilty of a breach of Unity, and so the sin of Schism lies at her door.

"This has been clearly shown by our best English divines; and a careful study of this proof is rendered requisite by the circumstances of these times."*

In the Church of England's Litany we pray, in words most suitable to our days, "From all sedition, privy conspiracy, and rebellion, from all false doctrine, heresy, and schism, from hardness of heart, and contempt of Thy Word and Commandment, *good Lord, deliver us.*"

Now, our Reformers, when including those words within the Prayer Book, were in brotherly communion with foreign Protestant non-Episcopal Churches, as shown by Dean Goode, and in the Zurich Letters and other works of the Parker Society. That communion was

---

* "Union with Rome," 8th ed., pp. 17, 18, 78, 79, 80.

based on a mutual agreement about the fundamental doctrines of the Christian religion, as
all important, whereas forms of outward government might vary, provided the case contained
the genuine jewels. On the other hand, our
Reformers had separated from the essentially
schismatic Church of Rome, on account of her
false doctrines and heresies, and because of
their regard for the supreme authority of the
Word of God, the "open Bible." But is there
no danger at this time lest certain Anglican
Bishops should follow suit with the Church of
Rome, in connection with projects for "Home
Reunion" between Churchmen and Nonconformists, as a preliminary to what is called "The
Reunion of Christendom," or " The Unity
[query Uniformity?] of Christendom"?—a phrase
which, with certain Anglican bishops, clergy,
and laity, really means a Reunion between
the Greek Church, the Romish Antichrist, and
the Church of England when sufficiently
Romanized by the Ritualists. Such danger
appears to be only too great.

The following remarks are taken from an
admirable paper* by the Rev. W. E. Rawstorne,

---

* Reprinted from the "Church of England Pulpit," 1889.

Hon. Canon of Manchester Cathedral, a paper deserving the careful attention of the laity, and, as the writer thinks, most deserving of wide circulation.

He says, "Reunion has become a subject of discussion in all Anglican assemblies. There have been movements in this direction in both the English Convocations, and in Australian and Canadian Synods; but the first attempt at naming definite terms, on which such Reunion might possibly be effected, was made by the General Assembly of the Protestant Episcopal Church of America in the year 1886. This body placed before the world a Resolution containing Four Articles. These were, in 1888, considered by a Committee of the Lambeth Conference of Anglican Bishops, and were, with certain modifications, reported upon favourably by that Committee, adopted unanimously by the assembled prelates, and embodied in their encyclical. Thus, there is a definite proposal before the world emanating from that body, which, from its position and peculiarities, is best qualified to take such a step. That proposal is contained in the following resolutions :—

"That, in the opinion of this Conference, the

following Articles supply a basis on which approach may be by God's blessing made towards Home Reunion :—

" (A.) The Holy Scriptures of the Old and New Testaments, as ' containing all things necessary to salvation,' and as being the rule and ultimate standard of faith.

" (B.) The Apostles' Creed, as the Baptismal Symbol ; and the Nicene Creed, as the sufficient statement of the Christian faith.

" (C.) The two Sacraments ordained by Christ Himself—Baptism and the Supper of the Lord—ministered with unfailing use of Christ's words of institution, and of the elements ordained by Him.

" (D.) The Historic Episcopate, locally adapted in the methods of its administration to the varying needs of the nations and peoples called of God into the unity of His Church."

After stating the fundamental principle on which these Four Articles are based, and re-marking upon them, he continues :— " We will . . . . only deal with those proposals which the Conference has thought politic to publish. Of the Four Articles, two (A. and C.) would be admitted without much discussion by the

great majority of Protestant Christians, and the
crucial points would be found to be (B and D)
the Creed and the Episcopate.

* * * * *

"Now, no one can dispute the right of Anglican
prelates to use within their own communion
that Creed of Constantinople (A.D. 381), or of
Chalcedon (A.D. 451), whichever it may be,
which passes under the name of the Nicene
Creed. It is a document of the fourth and
and fifth centuries, the work of men of that
period, and the embodiment of opinions
then prevailing; and as such it cannot be
elevated into a condition necessary for salvation,
or for communion, by a Church which professes
to found itself entirely on the original Christianity of the New Testament. The same must be
said of the so-called Apostles' Creed, an
occidental document, which, though its principal
lines are far more ancient, did not finally assume
its present form until the fifth, and possibly
even the sixth, century. No one objects to the
use of either of these formularies by members of
the Anglican Church, or wishes them to be expunged out of the Liturgy or Articles. The
Bishops can, without any objection or protest

H

from other religious bodies, hold, and recite, and teach, and recommend them, as much as they please, to their own members. But if they exalt into conditions of communion documents which are no part of the original deposit of Christian doctrine, they not only violate their own first principle, but also bar the Church door against many who have a right to enter, and are so far guilty of the division of Christendom.

"The other point which the Lambeth prelates hold to be essential, is what they call 'The Historic Episcopate.' Now, this is a very ambiguous term ; for no institution has suffered greater changes in the course of centuries than the Episcopal organizations of the Church. From the presbyter-bishops, holding co-ordinate authority over congregations in the Apostolic age, through the independent Episcopal τύραννοι whom the writer of the Ignatian letters desired to see established in every town, and the Byzantine system, prevailing in the time of Constantine and his successors, of a hierarchy of bishops, metropolitans, exarchs, patriarchs, modelled on Diocletian's secular organization of the empire, to the despotic Papacy of Innocent III., the distances traversed are enormous. Yet all these officials were bishops; and the institutions, of which they formed a part, are all included in historic Episcopacy. If the Anglican bishops are disposed to comprehend all these gradations under their phrase, they have prepared a ready way of reconciliation with the Presbyterians; for beyond all doubt, the first form of the historic Episcopate resembled the Presbyterian mode of organization more closely than any other existing form of Church Government. But we fear that this is precisely what they do not want to do. The first care of a hierarchy is always to maintain its own exclusive claims; nor have the majority of the prelates of the Anglican Church the slightest intention of accepting from their non-Episcopal fellow-Christians anything but unconditional surrender. They invite men, whose ministry has received the seal of the Great High Priest of the Christian profession in the bestowal upon them of the highest and noblest *charisms*, to come and crouch to them for those gifts of God which they have long ago received direct from Him, as if such gifts would come only through a bishop's hand. Is it to be expected that

H 2

any men will dishonour themselves, and their
ministry and the communities in which they
have lived and done noble service, by stooping
to such conditions? We are of opinion that
a better course is open, if only Anglican
prelates will submit to those facts of history
to which nominally they appeal."

*   *   *   *   *

Is not a plurality of professing Christian
Churches, frankly according to each other
perfect liberty in outward polity and internal
discipline, better for mankind than one world-
wide organization, which — History being
witness—would, like the Church of Rome,
degenerate into a terrific and all-enslaving
Spiritual Despotism? On that point, Canon
Rawstorne thus impressively speaks :—

" Under the providential government of the
world, the Christian Church has resolved itself
into several independent organizations. Instead
of this loss of organic unity being an evil to be
deplored, it is one of the greatest blessings ever
bestowed upon mankind. A strong hierarchy
cannot help being intolerant and tyrannical.
Now, as in the days of the great Popes, a
strongly-organized Catholic Church, spread over

all the world, and embracing all mankind, would be a colossal tyranny, against whose cage of iron bars all freedom of mind or of action would dash itself in vain. It is only the balance of power among independent religious communities which prevents persecution, guarantees freedom of thought and inquiry, and thereby supports in religion both subjected veracity and objective truth. The existence of separate organizations should be frankly acknowledged as a good, and not an evil—in fact, as an ordinance of God. And, then, abandoning the delusive dream of restoring an organic unity, which would be a curse and not a blessing, let Christian people make every effort to promote friendly feeling and co-operation, and, as the crown of all, intercommunion between Christian organizations and Christian individuals. If, instead of indulging in ambitious dreams of spiritual conquest and empire, the various Anglican assemblies and prelates would take as their aim the establishment of a friendly alliance of free Christian bodies, they would find their central position the best possible starting point from which to pursue that noble object; and Archbishop Benson might possibly find himself recognized by most Protestants, not quite as *papa alterius orbis*, but at least as *primus inter pares*.

"Nor should it ever be forgotten that the guilt of schism rests, not on those who claim and use that liberty which is the birthright of every Christian, but on those who advance exclusive claims, which nothing in original Christianity, or in the course of history, or in the present state of the Christian world, can justify—first on the asserters of the Papal despotism, and secondly on those who are attempting to revive the exclusive pretensions of Episcopacy.

"This is a matter for the consideration not only of clerical dignitaries, and ministers, and members of ecclesiastical assemblies. The laity of every denomination has the power and the duty to take an active part, not only in pro-moting, but also in actually effecting the reunion of the Church. Christian bodies, which admit each other's members to com-munion, are no longer in schism, although they be not members of the same organic body. If, therefore, the religious laity wish the Church to be reunited, let them communicate not only with the religious body, of which they profess to be actual members, but also with such other bodies as they believe to possess, in common with themselves, the vital parts of Christianity. At least, let them do so as far as those bodies will admit them ; for it is to be feared that, when this experiment is tried, no Christian body will be found to have a monopoly of intolerance. Encouraging examples may, however, be quoted, in which the experiment has been tried with success. There is, at least, one eminent lady, who not only selects her chaplains both from Episcopal and from Presbyterian communions, but also communicates in the little parish church of Crathie, as well as in the gorgeous fane of Windsor. And that lady--not the archbishop —is the supreme head of the Church of England. There is no inconsistency in such inter-communion. He who adopts this practice, professes that he himself is neither Episcopalian nor Presbyterian : he asserts his belief that neither Episcopacy nor Presbytery is a part of the essence of Christianity ; that each is a thing of human ordering and human choice ; and that a difference respecting them ought not to be allowed to keep Christian brethren asunder."

Now, first, *negatively*, has the Church of
Rome, during the centuries of her history preceding the Reformation of the sixteenth century,
or subsequently down to the present day, *raised
the nations under her spiritual and political
system to a higher condition of morality*, taking
the phrase in its widest sense, than has been
seen in Protestant countries, said by Romanists,
and others, to be under " destructive " and not
" constructive" influences, and lacking the
transcendent advantages claimed for Romanism ?
What intelligent, duly informed, and candid
student of history would support such a
contention ?

First, let us inquire whether or not her confessional system exercises such a superior influence on the morality of a population as its advocates assert to be the case.

The late Rev. Robert Seymour, in his able
and widely known book on " The Confessional,"
with reference to " The Primitive and Catholic
Forms of Absolution," and other matters, treats
to some extent of moral ethics in connection
with the Church of Rome's confessional system.
His book was published in 1870.

He deals with all subjects in a calm, fair,

logical, and judicial manner. "The argument in favour of the confessional as a deterrent from sin," he remarks, "opens out the inquiry whether, unless in exceptional cases, the confessional is found by experience really to prevent crime and vice.

" It is clear," as he says, " that from the very nature of confession, it comes *after the commission of the sin*, and therefore cannot be *a preventive of the sin*, except as against the repetition of the sin confessed.

" The inquiry," as to " whether, as a matter of fact, it does mitigate or lessen the amount of crime and vice, may," as he adds, " be made thus :—Let France, at the head of Roman Catholic civilization, be taken with all the supposed advantages of the confessional, and let England, at the head of Protestant civilization, be taken with all the supposed disadvantages of rejecting the confessional, and let these two populations be calmly and candidly compared in all the forms of crime and vice, and then let it be seen whether the practice of the confessional has made France more pure, and whether the rejection of the confessional has made England less pure—whether, in fact, the confessional has really proved itself a deterrent from vice and crime, and exercised in this respect a salutary influence on the morality of a population. There are great facilities for this inquiry, for, in France and in England alike, the most careful and elaborate returns are made year by year to their respective Governments, and published by them every year.

"From the latest official returns of the Governments of France and England for 1865 and 1866, a few figures," adds Mr. Seymour, "will enable the general reader to form his own judgment."

The writer can only in these pages give some of the results under two or three heads.

I. MURDER.

In France the convictions were :—

Murder	80
Attempts...	36
Assassination	117
Parricide and attempts	11
Infanticide and attempts ...	148
Poisoning and attempts... ...	16
Total	458

In England the convictions were :—

Murder ...	...	...	...	16
Attempts	...	...	...	8
Parricide ...	...	...	...	1
Infanticide	...	...	...	9
Total ...			...	34

Thus, in France, with a population of thirty-seven millions, there were about nine convictions for murder for every one in England, with a population for England and Wales of twenty-seven millions.

II. INFANTICIDE.

In France the convictions were :—

Infanticide	...	...	...	148
Homicide	...	...	...	143
Exposure ...	...	...	...	102
Total		...	...	395

In England the convictions were :—

Infanticide	...	...	...	9
Concealment	...	...	...	94
Abandoning	...	...	...	8
Total		...	...	111

III. VIOLATION.

" This," says Mr. Seymour, " most truly is amongst the most villainous of all crimes, and

exhibits a mingled atrocity and depravity, showing in a strong light the character of a population as regards morality. . . . . In France it is
nearly twice as prevalent as in England in proportion to the population."

Mr. Seymour then, from want of space, could
only show similar results as to the extent of
the highest of all crimes,* that of MURDER, in a
"comparison of England with other countries, as
Ireland, Belgium, Austria, Bavaria, Italy, &c."
He also gives similar results in comparing chief
" cities of Protestant England " with chief
" cities of Roman Catholic countries." He then
says, " Let the precise question at issue be now
remembered. These figures are not adduced to
insinuate, much less to prove, that the confessional is a source of crime or of vice. This
would be going beyond the necessities of the
present argument, which is, not that the confessional thus tends to evil, or that it generates
those evils, but only that it has not the
deterrent and preventive power which its advo-

---

* *Crimes* are offences against human laws. *Sin* is "the trans-
gression of the law of God " (1 John iii. 4). A Christian may be a
criminal in the eyes of human governments, or of intolerant and persecuting ecclesiastics, and yet be no sinner in the sight of God, but the
contrary (Acts xxiv. 1-14 ; John xv. 18-21, xvi. 1-3).

cates claim for it," who argue that, " it is so
salutary as a preventive that Roman Catholic
populations, among whom it is an established
institution, are more pure in their morals than
those Protestant populations who have rejected
it. The foregoing facts and figures, all taken
from official and governmental records, and not
from the worthless guesses of ignorant and
prejudiced travellers, who can never see beyond
the surface, are an answer annihilating this
argument of the advocates of the confessional."

Now, it must be remembered that, in addition to the confessional, for which so potent a
" moral force " is claimed, ROMANISM further
claims enormous and, indeed, immeasurable advantages over Protestant " heretics " and
" schismatics," who, in accordance with Rome's
CANON LAW, are *permanently* under the dread-
ful anathema of a Pope, whose predecessors
inculcated on Europe and elsewhere, in " historical continuity,"* that the Pope of Rome was "the
divinely appointed VICE-GOD, and so as God†"
on earth. Moreover, the late and the present

---

* On the "Historical continuity of the Church of England," see
Lord Halifax's remarks in the Appendix.

† Horæ Apocalypticæ," by the Rev. E. B. Elliott, 5th ed., vol.
iii., pp. 181-186. See the notes sustaining that terrible indictment.

Popes, having been officially declared to be personally INFALLIBLE, by the decree of the Vatican Council, their utterances *ex cathedrâ* have been blasphemously placed on a level with the Word of the living God; and, practically, from the withholding from Roman Catholics of the Bible without note or comment, the teaching of the Pope and his priesthood is placed above the Almighty and His holy Word.

Let us now take a peep at some of the other manifold spiritual agencies of the Church of Rome, to which an incomparable efficacy is attributed, quite unknown to Protestant Churches.

She has no less than seven Sacraments, all of them said to impart grace by virtue of their exercise by a priest, against only the two Sacraments mentioned in the New Testament, and adopted, therefore, by Protestants. She declares that her children reap vast spiritual benefit from the intercession of the Virgin Mary as co-mediatrix, and of the saints as co-mediators with Christ, while Protestants cannot have recourse to such help, because they find in God's Word that there is *only* "*one* God, and *one* Mediator between God and man, the Man Christ Jesus"

(1 Tim. ii. 5); she asserts that her Mass wafer, consecrated by a priest, imparts remission of the sins of the living and the dead, whereas Protestants are compelled to reject that dogma as idolatrous and blasphemous, partly because the Apostle Peter declares that Christ must remain in heaven, "*until* the times of restitution of all things" (Acts iii. 19-21); and St. Paul supports that truth from the Word of God, which says that Jesus Christ is to "sit on God's right hand, *until* He makes His enemies His footstool" (Heb. i. 13); and that Christ is only to leave heaven "the SECOND time without sin unto salvation" (Heb. ix. 27-28), to which the three Christian Creeds witness; and to adduce no other reasons, because the inspired Apostle declares that the object of the Lord's Supper *is not to make* His death, but, in a figure, to "show forth the Lord's death *till* He come" (1 Cor. xi. 23-26). Consequently, as Christ cannot have left heaven even once since He ascended to it, because "the Scripture cannot be broken," therefore His "real presence," as God-Man, or the *alone true* Christ of Scripture, never can have yet come down from heaven, and will not before His "*second* coming." But, if so,

what becomes of the claims of the imaginary
sacrificing priests, altars, and atoning Eucharistic sacrifices of Romanists and Ritualists ?*
In addition, Rome has absolving bishops and
priests, who profess to be as God in their tri-
bunal, and to forgive, not *offences against the
Church*, as used to be their vocation in *primitive* days, but, now, to forgive *sins against
God*, which Protestants reverentially believe to
be the prerogative of God alone for Christ's sake.
Rome claims salutary discipline, penances, and

---

* Some persons have thought that the Lord Jesus *has* left "the
right hand of God"—in other words, heaven—*before* the fulfilment of
the prophecies preceding His second advent. That would nullify
Scripture. They point to what occurred in connection with the
remarkable conversion of St. Paul (Acts ix. 1-18). But not only is
there not a word there to warrant the inference that our Lord Jesus
came down from heaven ; we have the Apostle's own explanation that,
as in the case of Stephen, it was a *vision of Christ in heaven*.
"O king Agrippa," he said, "I was not disobedient to the heavenly
vision" (Acts xxvi. 12-19).
   As regards the "false Christs" of the MASS and the Ritualistic Eucharistic sacrifice, it is never to be forgotten that our Saviour appealed
emphatically to His being, after His resurrection, "*the* SAME" Person
as before it, and VISIBLY so. He said, "Behold My hands and My
feet, that it is I Myself : handle Me, and see ; for a spirit hath not
flesh and bones, as ye see Me have" (Luke xxiv. 37-42). The angels
also have warned us that "*this* SAME Jesus, which is taken up from
you into heaven, shall so come in like manner as ye have seen Him go
into heaven" (Acts i. 11). Therefore an *invisible* Christ cannot be the
true Christ. Moreover, Christ Himself declared, and it is repeated
and amplified in various Scriptures, and embodied in the Creeds, that
when Christ comes it will be "in the clouds of heaven, with power
and great glory" (Matt. xxiv. 22-31).

scourgings—some of them very cruel; she boasts of what, if they are *not* true miracles, as seems clearly to be the case, must be the predicted "lying wonders" (2 Thess. ii. 3-12; compare Deut. xiii. 1-11). The Rev. Hobart Seymour, so widely known by his writings about the Jesuits and Romanism, thus informs us :

"There are superstitions connected with her graven images, some of which are called miraculous, I have seen them myself. There are superstitions connected with her pictures, her winking Madonnas and her weeping saints, I have examined them myself. There are superstitions connected with her relics, there are splinters of old bones, bits of skin, parings of nails, decayed teeth, all said to be Holy Relics of Holy Apostles—some of them have several heads, and others have some half-dozen arms, and as many legs." *   Mr. Seymour also witnessed the Romish ceremony of "*The Adoration of the Cross*" on Good Fridays. There is "a cross of wood on an altar, to which they

---

* The Protestant Character of the Church of England as it bears upon the Romanizing Movements within the Church" (Nisbet, 1865), p. 9.

I

say, ' Behold the wood of the Cross!' and
the response, is ' Come let us adore it!' and
the Pope, the cardinals, and all present kneel
and adore it." *

Then, still more, Rome provides helpful
rosaries, consecrated medals, and flagellating
whips, as if scoring the body could drive evil
out of the heart. She has numerous uses for
crucifixes and crosses. *For the cross is the
peculiar mark of the Latin Church.* Her congregations devoutly believe, on the word of their
priests, what is not taught in the Bible—that
making the sign of the cross charms away evil
spirits (in French, *ça chasse les demons*), and
is otherwise beneficial. She has gorgeous priests
and priestly processions in and out of her
Churches, and in the public streets, with imposing pomp and display, not precisely parallel,
perhaps, to the example of our Lord and His
Apostles, nor to His teaching (Matt. xi. 1-8,
xxiii.), and, to instance no more, she has holy
water, which, says a writer, " on numberless
occasions is used by the Romish Priesthood to

---

* "A Pilgrimage to Rome."—Are we not naturally reminded of the
worship of Nebuchadnezzar, his princes, the governors, the captains,
&c. ? (Dan. iii).

bless not only persons, but inanimate objects. It is believed to purify the air, heal distempers, cleanse the soul. . . . it is sprinkled on candles at Candlemas—upon palms on Palm Sunday . . . . upon beds, horses, meat, bells, fortifications, and cannon." *

How is it that, with all that immense array of agencies, and a good many more besides, including her army of monks and nuns, the Church of Rome's population throughout the world do not exhibit a morality in all its branches incomparably superior to the inhabitants of Protestant lands ?

A similar question might be put respecting extreme High Churchmen and Ritualists, with their transcendent spiritual claims and vast alleged superiority, as compared with the members of non-Episcopal Churches.

What, now, of the question, *Does* the Church of Rome, in her authoritative teaching and practices, shockingly outrage morality ? Too many voices past and present unite in giving a terrible affirmative reply to that question, which, however, can be but briefly treated in these pages.

---

* "The Faiths of the World," by the Rev. James Gardner, M.D., A.M., Vol. III.¹

From a tract on "The Moral Theology of the
Church of Rome,"* I give the following
extracts. They will speak for themselves :—
"We think it our duty to bring before the
public some of the *true* teaching of the Church
of Rome. To those who are not acquainted
with her history, doctrines, &c., she presents
herself in a most plausible manner—says she
is belied, slandered, &c. ; but when we come
to read her authorized works, we find there
the most ridiculous, immoral, filthy, and
abominable things that could possibly exist.
It is from one of these works that we shall
quote, viz., ' The Moral Theology of St.
Alphonso Maria de Liguori, Mech. 1845.'
*A decree concerning this theology was made
by the Sacred Congregation of Rites, and
was confirmed on May* 18, 1803, *by Pope
Pius VII.,* which declared that all the writings
of St. Alphonso, whether printed or inedited,
had been most rigorously examined, according
to the discipline of the Apostolic See, and
that not one word has been found ' *censuræ
dignum'!* It also declared that Liguori's Theology
had been *twenty years* rigorously discussed

---

* Published by the Protestant Alliance, 9, Strand, London.

with the rules of the decrees of *Pope Urban VIII. and Benedict XIV.,* and in the definitive judgment of the Sacred Congregation all agreed '*voce concordi, unanimi consensu, una voce, unanimiter.*'—*Dublin Calendar* for 1845, p. 167. Thus the Church of Rome has declared that in Liguori's Theology there is not one word worthy of censure; and, therefore, it is the true teaching of the Church of Rome!

"Liguori *was made a Saint of the Church of Rome on Trinity Sunday, May* 26, 1839!

"We may premise that Liguori holds the probable system, and his Theology is written according to it.

*　　*　　*　　*　　*

"On Equivocation, Liguori says, 'A confessor can affirm, EVEN WITH AN OATH, that HE DOES NOT KNOW A SIN heard in confession, by *understanding as man*, NOT *as the minister of Christ*, as St. Thomas 2, 2, 9, 70, art. 1, ad. 1, Lug. disp. 22, teach, (who, however, n. 75, explains, in another manner, that word that he *does not know it through a knowledge which is useful for answering*).'—*Id.*, vol. ii., n. 153, p. 319, *ibid.*

"Again—' A poor man, absconding with goods for his support, can answer the judge THAT HE HAS NOTHING. *Salm.* n. 140.'—*Id.*, vol. ii., n. 158, p. 321, *ibid.* Again—' It is asked, whether an adulteress can deny adultery to her husband,' and Liguori answers this proposition, ' If sacramentally she confessed adultery, she can answer, I am innocent of this crime, because by confession it was taken away ? ' "—Vol. ii. n., 162, p. 322.

Gury affirms the same proposition (Vol. ii., p. 355). See " The Doctrines of Jesuits and Roman Catholic Writers on Murder, Theft, Perjury, and other Crimes," by Arthur H. Guinness, M.A., Secretary to the Protestant Alliance, 9, Strand, London, W.C.

*   *   *   *   *

" Again — ' A servant can, *according to his own judgment*, COMPENSATE HIMSELF FOR HIS LABOUR, if *he*, without doubt, judge that he was deserving of a larger stipend.' — *Id.*, vol. iii., n. 524, p. 246.

"Again—' Whether it be a mortal sin to steal a small piece of a relic ? There is no doubt but that *in the district of* ROME *it is a mortal sin,*' &c. : ' OTHERWISE, Croix probably says (with

others) if any one should steal any *small* thing
OUT of the district of Rome,' &c.—*Id.*, vol. iii.,
n. 256, *ibid.* This seems rather curious doctrine, that a *theft* should be sin in one place but
not in another!

"Liguori admits that the confessional has pro-
duced immorality. He says, 'Oh, how may
Priests who before were innocent on account of
similar attractions (of women) which began in
the spirit, HAVE LOST BOTH GOD AND THEIR
SOUL.'—*Id.*, *Praxis Confessarii*, vol. ix., n. 119,
c. 8, p. 104, *ibid.* Again—'*Oh, how many
Confessors have lost their own souls, and those
of their penitents*, on account of some negligence
in this respect,' viz., hearing the confessions of
women.—*Id.*, vol. ix., c. 10, n. 193, p. 145, *ibid.*

"Again—'Whether a confessor, soliciting to
immodest actions which are only venial, should
be denounced? The first opinion is affirmative,
&c.; but the second *more probable opinion is
negative.*'—*Id.*, vol. vii., lib. iv., n. 682, p. 167,
ibid.

"He says, under the head of 'Restitution,'
that a ravisher, if he be a great man, is not
bound to marry a woman if she is much inferior
to him in station, even though he has *promised*

marriage to her with an oath !!—Id., vol. iii., lib. vi., n. 643, p. 530, *ibid.*

" Is not Rome fully proved to be the mother of harlots and abominations of the earth from her own authorized standards? Let us, therefore, cling to the *only* sufficient Rule of *Faith and Practice*, the Bible. ' To the Law and to the Testimony : if they do not speak according to this word, it is because there is no light in them.'—Isaiah, chap. viii. 20. Let any parent become acquainted with the abominations of Dens' and Liguori's Theology on the Confessional, and he would, with pleasure, exchange its horrors for the persecutions of heresy, and prefer the stake for his wife or daughter to the racks of that moral inquisition to which she is there bound to submit ! Here is the mighty secret of this inquisitorial cell of iniquity and of death. It is not the system of licentiousness, awful as that is, but the awful and illimitable tyranny it upholds.—*Elliott's Delineation of Romanism*, book ii., p. 202. Let us, then, in every legitimate manner that we can, oppose the spread of that earthly, sensual, and devilish system. Let us energize for the spread of Christianity and the downfall of error ; and once more, the great and rapid increase of Romanism calls out to every true follower of the Lord Jesus Christ to arise, for now 'it is high time to awake out of sleep.'—Rom. xiii. 11.

" The Word of God, referring to Rome, says, 'Come out of her, my people, that ye be not partakers of her sins, and that ye receive not of her plagues.'—Rev. xviii. 4. It is, then, our duty, not only to come out of Romanism into the light and liberty of Protestanism, but it is also our duty to keep it from our Constitution, our doctrines, and our Churches, in whatever shape it may come, be it in the appearance of Processions, Genuflections, Tractarianism, Decorations, Crosses, &c. Rome will not hear of *equality*; that is only a specious pretext for acquiring power ; she will never rest till she has obtained *absolute supremacy !* "

In one of the valuable " Monthly Letters of the Protestant Alliance," drawn up by Mr. Guinness, for September 1880, he gives the following extracts from M. Charles Sauvestre's work, which,* as will be seen, more than confirm the statements in the official returns quoted by Mr. Hobart Seymour. How far they illustrate

---

* Sur Les Genoux de l'Eglise, Paris, 1880.

certain features of spiritual Babylon given in
Rev. xvii. 1-5 must be left to the reader.

Our eternally unchangeable God, the Holy,
Holy, Holy One, in His infinite love, goodness,
and wisdom, has given to mankind the sacred
institution of marriage, and has caused to be
written concerning it, " Marriage is honourable in all, and the bed undefiled : but whoremongers and adulterers God will judge " (Heb.
xiii. 4). It is, under God's blessing, a holy safe-
guard from incontinence and Satan's temptations (1 Cor. vii. 1-13). Moreover, the clergy
in particular are enjoined to be married men
(1 Tim. iii. 1-12). But if the laws and commandments ordained of God for the good of
man be despised, and natural laws are wilfully
violated by fallen and presumptuous men, the
consequences, as history in all ages, and that of
the Church of Rome in particular, only too
abundantly prove, must be more terrible than
words could express, or than could be made
known for public perusal (Compare Jer. ii. 8-19 ;
Rom. i. 18-32 ; Gal. vi. 7, 8).

The following are the quotations in Mr.
Guinness' Monthly Letter (official journal of
that date). It states, " ' Of all the liberal pro-

fessions, physicians have furnished the least
number of those who have been brought before
the legal tribunals. The number is so small that
it is impossible to make a comparison with the
other classes. In ten years, from 1829 to 1840,
we reckon that there were 41,679 males, of
above 25 years of age, who were brought up before the courts ; amongst these were 35 priests,
33 advocates, 9 attorneys, 75 notaries, 66
officers, and not a single physician.' M. Wahu
remarks, ' That in the exercise of their profes-
sions physicians constantly receive the confid-
ences of young and old, married and single, and
yet no physician has been brought before the
legal tribunals charged with an offence against
morality.' But the physicians are not compelled
to take upon themselves vows of celibacy, but are
respected as husbands and fathers, honoured in
their family ties, whilst the priest is compelled
to store his mind with the immoral pollution
found in the writings of Liguori, and of such
Jesuits as Sanchez, Moullet, Busembaum, and
Gury."

" On the part of the priesthood," [of Rome]
remarks the Rev. Hobart Seymour, " the
preparation for the confessional forms a large

portion of clerical education. The candidate must be initiated, so far as theory is concerned, into every kind of sin, every form of vice, every phase of impurity, and every way in which the vilest passions of our fallen nature can be indulged. . . . . To this study they have given the name of 'moral theology.' And the books written with a view to these studies in all the seminaries for the priesthood are of such a nature that they revolt and disgust the laity even to loathing at their filthiness and indecency. *It is impossible to expose them to the indignant feelings of a Christian nation like this, as the very act of exposing them would be the mischievous circulation of their hideous contents.* When on a late occasion * an attempt at exposing them was made by publishing extracts from them, by which the public could be made acquainted with their nature, the righteous laws of our land interposed in the interest of public morals to prevent the circulation of such infamy, and *the judges of the land pronounced it illegal under the laws which prohibit 'indecent publications.'* Yet in the Church of Rome the study of these is thought necessary to prepare

---

* The remarks above were published in 1670.

the youthful student in its colleges for the duties of the confessional. It is not here intended to convey—it would not be true—that every confessor inflicts this knowledge on his penitent, nor yet that every penitent is tortured by a process * savouring of all this, but it is designed merely to convey the matter of fact that a course of study of such a nature that no experience in the public schools, in the universities, in the barracks of this land, can convey an adequate idea, *is imposed upon all candidates for the priesthood in the Church of Rome, as a necessary preparation for the duties of the confessional.* A Christian may well weep in pity and compassion over young minds exposed to all the defilement of such studies."

Further, Mr. Seymour remarks, " In Roman Catholic countries the Catechisms for children between nine and twelve years of age, at which time they prepare them for their first confession and first communion, familiarize the children with the names and nature of the most odious and revolting vices, to such an extent that

---

* Of the nature and effects of such exquisite torture to a delicate and ignorant mind, Mrs. Richardson treats with feminine reticence, but in most harrowing terms, in her "Personal Experience of Roman Catholicism."

adults in this Protestant country are shocked beyond expression at such precociousness in the knowledge of evil. These Catechisms are the first suggestion of such sins to their minds —the first initiation in sin to their young and innocent minds. As they advance in years, these manuals contain further developments of such subjects, in order, as it is alleged, that they may more fully analyse and examine their own thoughts and feelings, so as to be enabled to render a more full and precise confession. . . . . When, after reading ["the most reserved and chastened of these manuals "] *the young maiden kneels before her unmarried confessor, and shrinks in the sensitive delicacy of her nature from entering on such subjects in such a presence,* she is liable at once to be *forced* into it. *The threat of refusing absolution* without a full confession compels her compliance.* Her scruples and her delicacy must be dismissed, and the unmarried priest—if he desire it— must be told all the movements and thoughts and feelings of the penitent. It ought not to be said or thought that every priest thus

---

* Compare Mrs. Richardson's "Personal Experience." (Morgan & Scott.)

questions his penitents, or that every penitent is so questioned ; but only *that every priest has the power and every penitent has the liability to all this process,* by which all sense of female delicacy and feminine modesty and womanly reserve are annihilated in the presence of a priest."*

Now, bearing in mind the fearful admission of the ruinous consequences of the Confessional System, made by no less a person than the Canonised Saint and Roman Casuist, LIGUORI, whose writings, as we have seen, have received the official imprimatur of the " Sacred Congregation " of Rome, and the entire approval of several Popes, *as " not containing one word worthy of censure,"* bearing in mind, also, that even some extracts from the Manuals of Liguori and others—such as Bailly and Delahogne (from whose treatises Mr. Seymour gives a few extracts in Latin)—were condemned by our judges as unfit for publication and circulation amongst the public ; and bearing further in mind that " every priest has the power and every penitent has the liability to all this process," is it any wonder that, from time to

---

* "The Confessional," pp. 178-189.   Italics not in the original.

time, Roman Catholic laymen have prohibited their wives and daughters from going to confess to their unmarried priests ?

Were the laity generally of the Church of Rome fully aware of the real teaching connected with the confessional, and of the disastrous evils to be reasonably expected *from the fruits of such a tree*—evils which as Liguori, and others in the Church of Rome's history, have testified as having actually occurred—would not that laity, as one man, unite to preserve their wives and daughters, and every woman, high or low, from the bare *possibility* of such frightful results ?

And if the Protestant constituencies of England and Ireland were similarly enlightened, would they not be effectually moved indignantly to insist that, unless such foul blots were at once removed from the imperative Educational Code at such State-paid colleges as Maynooth, *such poisonous seminaries should be immediately disendowed*, and not another shilling of Protestant money be wickedly allowed to maintain a system allowed by its own Popes, Sacred Congregations, and theological saints to possess features so unscriptural, so anti-Christian, so fraught with deadly perils ?

Would not the *duly enlightened* laity of the Protestant Church of England do likewise? Would not the laity of *all* parties within our Church act so as to preserve their families from the similar teaching propagated, and the Romish confessional perils risked by Ritualistic so-called "priests" poisoning and corrupting amongst us; and, as in the case of Romish priests of the predicted Apostasy—"creeping into houses, and leading captive silly women laden with sins, led away with divers lusts, ever learning, and never able to come to the knowledge of the truth"? (2 Tim. iii. 1-7).

Manuals such as those alluded to by Mr. Seymour *are now circulated* by such wolves in sheep's clothing. One, says an able writer, called "The Priest in Absolution," dealing "with the subject of confession from the Romish point of view, for the instruction of Anglican clergy in the practice of confession, and compiled from Romish works, directs the same polluting questions to be put to the penitent that are inculcated by the Romish theologians."

That abominable production was strongly denounced in the House of Lords. Of course it

K

is reprobated by every right-minded bishop, clergyman, and layman.

Many years ago, the writer was led in Canada to challenge the Roman Catholic priests to dare to translate from the Latin into English, and to submit to public opinion, certain extracts from Liguori and other standard theologians whose writings were used *permissu superiorum.* That challenge was not accepted. IT NEVER WILL BE ACCEPTED. For, has not HE who "is the Truth" unanswerably said, "Every one that doeth evil hateth the light, neither cometh to the light, lest his deeds be reproved. But he that doeth truth cometh to the light, that his deeds may be made manifest, that they are wrought in God"? (John iii. 19-21).

In the *Sussex Daily News* for October 21, 1890, there appeared, in reply to a letter signed "M. A. Fluder," advocating the use of the confessional in strong terms, another letter signed "John Thornberry," which contains a similar challenge to the Ritualists of Brighton. His letter closes thus :— "Well, Sir, I am but a poor man, yet I will pay for the use of the Dome for one evening, if the Curate of St. Bartholomew's will come and read and translate

into English, in the presence of his fellow-towns-
men, portions of those books which he would
have us believe are so salutary, and without the
use of which society must collapse. Surely this
is not too much, in all fairness, to ask him to do,
and then the men of Brighton will be able to
judge whether Mr. Thompson has any right to
minister in any Church in this highly-favoured
land."

As regards Ritualism generally, is it not high
time that all true and faithful laymen in our
Church should unite cordially and resolutely
together, in some mutual aid association, to
support and help each other in parishes where
they are driven away, by Ritualists or by the
" fearful " and compromising amongst Evangelical clergymen, from their parish church?
Should they not zealously help each other to
provide mission rooms, or other accommodation
in barns, if necessary, or, in drawing-rooms, or
elsewhere, where our God and Saviour could be
worshipped in spirit and in truth, and in the
use of our holy, reverential, spiritual, and
wondrously comprehensive Liturgy, or with
such kindred modifications thereof as may be
found in some localities desirable? Union is

strength, and is it not written, "Look not every man on his own things, but every man also on the things of others"? (Phil. ii. 1-11).

On the vital and fundamental doctrine of Justification before God, through faith in the finished work of Christ, without any meritorious works of our own subjoined thereto, though such writing and saving faith in Christ "worketh by love" to Him, and through Him, brings forth a holy life and good works abundantly (Rom. iv., v. 1-11 ; John xv. 1-14, xix. 30 ; 1 Cor. i. 30, 31 ; Col. ii. 8-15 ; Gal. v. 1-6, 16-26 ; James ii. 14-26), the "judicious" HOOKER witnesses in his grand style* against the unscriptural and anti-Christian teaching of the Church of Rome, partly by faith in Christ, partly by faith in the Virgin Mary and the Saints, partly by faith in the multitudinous contrivances of which specimens have been given in these pages, partly by our own meritorious works, all jumbled up with Christ's complete and "FINISHED" work (John xix. 30). Hence, Rome's very *religiousness*, which is not the

---

* In his noble Discourse on Justification.

BIBLE's religion, all the while flagrantly dis-
honours our blessed Lord and only Saviour.

First, let us note well Hooker's very
weighty words as follows :—" If any man
think that I seek to varnish their opinions [in
the Church of Rome] to set the better foot of a
lame cause foremost, let him know that since
I began thoroughly to understand their meaning, I have found their halting greater than
perhaps it seemeth to them which know not
the deepness of Satan, as the beloved Divine
speaketh.* For, although this be proof
sufficient that they do not directly deny the
foundation of Faith ; yet, if there were no other
leaven in the lump of their doctrine but this,
this were sufficient to prove that their doctrine
is not agreeable to the foundation of Christian
Faith."

Further on, he thus protests against the
bewildering and soul-destroying " MAZE " [or
labyrinth] which, as he remarks, " the Church
of Rome doth cause her followers to tread."

" The first receipt of Grace in their Divinity
is the first Justification ; the increase thereof,
the second Justification. As Grace may be

---

* Rev. ii. 20-23.

increased by the merit of good works, so it may
be diminished by the demerit of sins venial, it
may be lost by mortal sin. For as much therefore as it is needful in the one case to repair, in
the other to recover the loss which is made: the
infusion of Grace hath her sundry after-meals ;
for the which cause they make many ways to
apply the infusion of Grace. It is applied to
Infants, through Baptism, without either Faith
or Works, and in them really it taketh away
original sin, and the punishment due unto it.
It is applied to Infidels and wicked men in the
first Justification, through Baptism without
Works, yet not without Faith ; and it taketh
away both sins actual and original together,
with all whatsoever punishment eternal or
temporal thereby observed. Unto such as have
attained the first Justification, that is to say,
the first receipt of Grace, it is applied farther
by good works to the increase of former Grace,
which is the second Justification. If they work
more and more, Grace doth more increase, and
they are more and more justified. To such as
diminished it by venial sins, it is applied by
Holy-water, *Ave Mary's*, Crossings, Papal
Salutations, and such like, which serve for

reparations of Grace decayed. To such as have lost it through mortal sin, it is applied by the Sacrament (as they term it) of Penance : which Sacrament hath force to confer Grace anew, yet in such sort, that being so conferred, it hath not altogether so much power, as at the first. For it only cleanseth out the stain or guilt of sin committed, and changeth the punishment eternal into a temporal satisfactory punishment here, if time do serve ; if not, hereafter to be endured, except it be lightened by Masses, Works of Charity, Pilgrimages, Fasts, and such like ; or else shortened by pardon for a term, or by plenary pardon quite removed, and taken away. This is the mystery of the man of sin. This *Maze* the Church of *Rome* doth cause her followers to tread, when they ask her the way to Justification. I cannot stand now to unrip this building, and sift it piece by piece ; only I will pass it by in few words, that that may befall *Babylon* in the presence of that which God hath builded, as happened unto *Dagon* before the Ark." *

Hooker then shows how much more perilous to souls is the system of ANTICHRIST, or the

---

* See Wordsworth, pp. 44 45.

Church of Rome of 2 Thess. ii., and Rev. xiii.
1-9, than open infidelity.

"Infidels and Heathen men," he says, "were
not so godless, but that they may, no doubt,
cry God mercy, and desire in general to have
their sins forgiven. To such as deny the
foundation of Faith there can be no Salvation
(according to the ordinary course which God
doth use in saving men) without a particular
repentance of that error. The *Galatians*
thinking that, unless they were circumcised,
they could not be saved, overthrew the foundation of Faith directly : therefore if any of them
did die so persuaded, whether before or after, they
were told by their Errors. Their end is dread-
ful ; there is no way with them but one, death
and condemnation. For the Apostle speaketh
nothing of men departed, but faith generally of
all. *If ye be circumcised, Christ shall profit
you nothing. Ye are abolished from Christ,
whosoever are justified by the Law; ye are
fallen from Grace, Gal. v.* Of them in the
Church of *Rome*, the reason is the same. For
whom Antichrist hath seduced, concerning
them did not *St. Paul* speak long before, they
received not the word of truth, that they might

be saved ? Therefore God would *send them strong delusions to believe lies, that all they might be damned which believe not the truth, but had pleasure in unrighteousness.* And *St. John, all that dwell upon the earth shall worship Him, whose names are not written in the Book of Life, Apoc. xiii.* Indeed many in former times, as their Books and Writings do yet shew, held the foundation, to wit, Salvation by Christ alone, and therefore might be saved. God hath always had a Church amongst them, which firmly kept His saving truth. *As for such as hold with the Church of* ROME, *that* we cannot be saved by Christ alone without works, *they do not only by a circle of consequence, but directly, deny the foundation of Faith ; they hold it not, no, not so much as by a thread.*"*

From the deeply interesting " Memorials of the Right Reverend Charles Pettit McIlvaine, D.D., D.C.L., late Bishop of Ohio, is taken the following beautiful delineation of the Scriptural way of justification by HOOKER, forming part of "the important series of extracts " given by the

---

* " On the Laws of Ecclesiastical Politie," by Richard Hooker, 1682, pp. 94, 95, 500, 510, 511. The words from " As for such " to the end are not italicized in the original.

Bishop in his "great work"—as Canon Carns so truly terms it—on "RIGHTEOUSNESS BY FAITH," and in which that admirable Bishop says, "We have now presented a chain of testimony to the great Protestant and Gospel doctrine of Justification by the *imputed* righteousness of Christ, that righteousness consisting in Christ's *active* obedience in fulfilling the Law, as well as in His *passive* in suffering its penalty ; that righteousness applied, embraced, or apprehended only by faith ; and faith in this act, though necessarily a lively and working faith, and working by love, yet not effectual in this application of Christ's righteousness, *because* it is a virtue, or work of love, but simply because it is the empty hand of an unworthy beggar reached out unto and taking hold of Christ " (pp. 391, 392).

Here now is Hooker's clear and beautiful description of Justification :—

" Christ," he says, " hath merited righteousness for as many as are found in Him. In Him God findeth us if we be faithful, for by faith we are incorporated into Christ. Then, although in ourselves we be altogether sinful and unrighteous, yet even the man which is impious in

himself, full of iniquity, full of sin, him being
found in Christ through faith, and having his
sin remitted through repentance, him God
beholdeth with a gracious eye, putteth away
his sin by not imputing it, taketh quite away
the punishment due thereunto by pardoning it,
and accepteth him in Jesus Christ as perfectly
righteous, as if he had fulfilled all that was
commanded him in the Law; shall I say more
perfectly righteous than if he had fulfilled the
whole Law. I must take heed what I say; but
the Apostle saith, '*God made Him to be sin for
us, who knew no sin, that we might be made the
righteousness of God in Him.*' Such we are in
the sight of God the Father, as is the very Son
of God Himself. Let it be counted folly, or
frenzy, or fury, whatsoever, it is our comfort
and our wisdom; we care for no knowledge in
the world but this, that man hath sinned and
God hath suffered; that God hath made Himself the Son of Man, and that men are made
the righteousness of God. You see, therefore,
that the Church of Rome, in teaching justification by inherent grace, doth pervert the truth
of Christ; and that by the hands of the
Apostles we have received otherwise than she

teacheth. Now, concerning the righteousness of sanctification, we deny it not to be inherent ; we grant that unless we work we have it not ; only we distinguish it as a thing different in nature from the righteousness of justification. We are righteous, the one way, by the faith of Abraham, the other way, except we do the works of Abraham we are not righteous. Of the one, St. Paul, ' *To him that worketh not, but believeth, faith is accounted for righteousness ;*' of the other, St. John, ' *Qui facit justitiam, justus est.*' He is righteous which worketh righteousness. Of the one, St. Paul doth prove, by Abraham's example, that we have it of faith without works ; of the other, St. James, by Abraham's example, that by works we have it, and not only by faith. St. Paul doth plainly sever these two parts of Christian righteousness one from the other ; for in the sixth to the Romans thus he writeth, ' *Being freed from sin, and made servants to God, ye have your fruit in holiness, and the end everlasting life.*' *Ye are made free from sin, and made servants unto God :* this is the righteousness of justification ; *ye have your fruit in holiness ;* this is the righteousness

of sanctification.   By the one, we are interested
in the right of inheriting ; by the other, we are
brought to the actual possession of eternal bliss,
and so the end of both is everlasting life
(Sect. 6).

"We ourselves do not teach Christ alone,
excluding our own faith unto justification;
Christ alone, excluding our own works unto
sanctification ; Christ alone, excluding the one
or the other unnecessary unto salvation.   It is a
childish cavil wherewith in the matter of justification our adversaries do so greatly please
themselves, exclaiming that we tread all Christian virtues under our feet, and require nothing
in Christians but Faith ; because we teach that
Faith alone justifieth ; whereas by this speech
we never meant to exclude either Hope or
Charity from being always joined as inseparable
mates with Faith in the man that is justified ;
or works from being added as necessary duties
required at the hands of every justified man ;
but to show that Faith is the only hand which
putteth on Christ unto justification ; and Christ
the only garment which being so put on covereth
the shame of our defiled natures, hideth the im-
perfection of our works, preserveth us blameless

in the sight of God, before whom otherwise the weakness of our Faith were cause sufficient to make us culpable, yea, to shut us out from the kingdom of Heaven, where nothing that is not absolute can enter" (Sect. 31).*

The faith of that holy Bishop, through the grace of God, stood him in blessed and all-conquering stead in the prospect of "the supreme moment" of our transitory days on earth, awaiting each and all of us. In the "Memorials" it is thus given by Canon Carns.

Bishop McIllvaine's Peaceful Anticipation of soon Dying.—"Last Friday, June 3rd," [1859] says the Bishop, " the Convention elected an Assistant Bishop, the Rev. G. T. Bedell. The choice was gratifying to me because of the good man elected, and because he was elected by such strength of vote as showed the determination of the Diocese to sustain the policy, the doctrine, &c., which have marked my Episcopate. The Lord be praised for this. In the prospect of being soon removed from hence, it relieves my mind to think that my office will fall to one in whose piety, knowledge

* "Memorials," pp. 390, 391, 392.

of the truth, wisdom, and faithfulness I have so
much confidence. Now, Gracious Master, order
all influences bearing on the mind of that brother,
so that he may see what his duty is, and come
to us heartily and devotedly, if Thou dost
approve the choice. But all this, how it speaks
to me of my nearness to my last week on earth
and my departure hence ! I expect to die suddenly—most likely it will be by sudden stroke
of insensibility. Blessed Lord, I have no request
to make in that regard, but whatever the mode,
and whenever the time, *Thou* wilt be with me.
I trust Thy grace to be sufficient for me, to be
my help, my need, *a very present help.* I
earnestly desire to glorify Thee by a lively hope
at the last. But if it please Thee that I go too
suddenly to do that, Thy will be done. I am
amazed at the little dread and feeling of sadness
that I have in surveying, as so near my end, and
in realizing, as I do, how very uncertain is each
day. I can think and speak of going, as it were,
a pleasing journey home ; the darkness of the
valley is overlooked in the bright vision of the
blessedness beyond. The prospect seems familiar.
All there seems as it is but for a day or two.
Eternity—the home of the people of God—

stands always in sight. I feel that I have a home and treasure there. And why? Simply, dear blessed Jesus, because Thou art there—my life, my refuge, my righteousness, all my hope; and I trust I am Thine, in Thee, a true believer, a living branch of Thee, the Vine. Whenever I think of eternity, instantly all my thoughts and hopes and affections run to Thee. O Lord, give me more of Thy Spirit of life, that I may have more of this witnessing that I am Thine. Be indeed my inheritance. ' Let me not be ashamed of my hope.' Jesus, hold me up when I go down to death, and fill me with the joy of Thy presence."

Oh, dear reader, may the Lord God of all grace grant to you and to me, for Christ's precious sake, the fulness of such a beautiful and and effectual faith, and such heavenly yearnings and anticipations!

To readers of Miss Marsh's very interesting Memoir of her venerable and widely-loved father, Dr. Marsh, the following expressive lines by the celebrated Greek scholar, Dr. Valpy, which, as we learn, were essentially blessed to an old Peninsular general officer, who read them when visiting the late Earl of Roden, and have been

helpful to others, may be thought a suitable
accompaniment to the happy experience of
Bishop McIlvaine.   The lines are as follows :—

" In peace let me resign my breath,
  And Thy salvation see,
My sins deserve eternal death,
  But Jesus died for me."

THOUGHTS ON THE ROMISH MASS

AND

The Equivalent Eucharistic Sacrifice of the Ritualists.

Our blessed Lord and Master, before His ascension to heaven there to " sit at the right hand of God" (Heb. i. 8-12 ; 1 Peter iii. 22 ; Col. iii. 1), declared, both in plain speech and by parable, that he *would remain* ABSENT *from this earth* until this Gentile Dispensation or " times of the Gentiles be fulfilled,"* and the time arrived for the restoration of His people Israel to their own land, their conversion, the elevation of Jerusalem into the capital and "joy of the whole earth," and Christ's introduction of their long promised period of peace, security and holiness never from that time to be interrupted.

---

* Amongst many passages see Hosea i. 10, 11 ; Ezek. xxxvi. 24-38 ; Isa. lxv ; Jer. xxxii. 37-44, xxxiii. ; Hos. iii. 4, 5 ; Zech. xii., xiv. ; Rom. xi. 25-33.

His absence would continue for "a long while,"*—long, that is, in the estimation of men, but not long before the Lord with whom "one day is as a thousand years, and a thousand years as one day," as the Apostle Peter, by prophetic anticipation, replies to "the last day scoffers, walking after their own lusts, and saying, Where is the promise of His coming? for since the fathers fell asleep, all things continue as they were from the beginning of the creation."†

Our Lord said to His disciples, "The poor always ye have with you, but Me you have not always."‡

Again, "It is expedient for you that I go away; for if I go not away, the Comforter will not come unto you; but if I depart, I will send Him unto you."||

So, whilst Christ, *as God-Man*, was in heaven until His second coming, the Holy Spirit, in

---

* Matt. xxv. 14-19. On that parable Matthew Henry observes:—
"Many in the Apostles' times imagined that the day of the Lord was at hand, but it is not so. Christ as to us seems to tarry, and really doth not (Heb. x. 37). There is good reason for the Bridegroom's tarrying, there are many intermediate counsels and purposes to be accomplished : the elect must all be called in, God's patience must be manifested and the saints' patience tried, the harvest of the earth must be ripened, and so must the harvest of heaven too. But though Christ tarry past our time, He will not tarry past the due time."

† 2 Peter iii. 1-11.   ‡ John xii. 8. || John xvi. 7 ; xiv. 26.

His absence, was to guide, govern, and comfort them, as Christ had done whilst with them. His Deity neither comes nor goes. But His language is accommodated, as it frequently is in the Bible, to our finite faculties, and our habits of thought. He is Himself the Divine " I AM." He could say, " Before Abraham was, I AM."* Therefore, as God, Christ could say, " Am I a God at hand, saith the Lord, and not a God afar off? . . . . Do not I fill heaven and earth? saith the Lord."† He could promise to be with every believer in Him by his Holy Spirit, as He said, " Where two or three are gathered together in My name, there am I in the midst of them."‡ But as " perfect Man " Christ's manhood, being a creature, cannot be endowed with *ubiquity,* which is the sole prerogative of God. It would be to confound the two distinct natures in Christ, and by destroying His humanity, it would accomplish the subtle denial that Christ came " *in the* FLESH," that is, with *a true and natural* HUMANITY, which is the essential mark of the predicted ANTICHRIST.§

---

* John viii. 56-59. † Jer. xxiii. 23, 24. ‡ Matt. xviii. 20.

§ 1 John iv. 1-3; 2 John 7-11. The R.V. makes the article emphatic, and reads "*the* antichrist."

Once more, our Lord said, " I go to prepare a place for you. And if I go to prepare a place for you, I will come again, and receive you unto Myself, that where I am, there ye may be also." *

Now, *when* was *the real presence* of Christ, as God-Man, to come again to our earth, and *in what way?*

First, as to the time.

On His ascension into heaven, God said unto the Son, " Sit on My right hand, UNTIL I make Thine enemies Thy footstool," † But that event has not yet been accomplished. Therefore, Christ cannot even once have left heaven since His ascension thither.

Again, the Apostle Peter said unto the men of Israel, " [The Lord] shall send Jesus Christ, which before was preached unto you ; whom the heaven must receive, UNTIL *the times of restitution of all things*, which God hath spoken by the mouth of all His holy prophets since the world began."‡

---

* John xiv. 1-3. Dean Goode, in his most valuable work on the Eucharist, quotes several of the Scriptures on our Lord's absence, as completely contradicting the teaching of Romanists and Ritualists on "*the* real presence " dogma.

† Heb. i. 8-13.   ‡ Acts iii. 19-21.

Now, clearly, that period has not yet arrived, as Bengel and other commentators elucidate. It includes the restoration of the Jews, *the destruction of the previously " consumed "* Antichrist,[*] whose Romish *germs* of Mariolatry, the Primacy, Intolerance, Apostolic Succession, &c., were *" already working "* in *the days of our Lord and His Apostles.*[†]

Therefore, on that Scripture ground also, our Lord and Saviour has not yet left heaven.

Again, it is written, "As it is appointed unto men once to die, but after this the judgment; so Christ was once offered to bear the sins of many; and unto them that look for Him shall He appear the SECOND time without sin unto salvation.[‡]

Not until His SECOND advent, then, is our Redeemer to come down from heaven. To that important truth, the three Creeds, the *Te Deum*, and the *Agnus Dei* at the end of the Church of England's Communion Service, unite in bearing witness.

---

* 2 Thess. ii. 3-8.

† Mark ix. 33-42; Luke ix. 49, 50; Matt. xii. 46-50; Matt. xx. 20-28; 3 John 9, 10.

‡ Heb. ix. 27, 28; " Without sin," that is, no longer bearing our sins, but coming in glory.

Moreover, in the Collect for the third Sunday
in Advent, we pray, " O Lord Jesu Christ
. . . . grant . . . . . that at Thy SECOND
COMING to judge the world, we may be found an
acceptable people in Thy sight, who livest and
reignest with the Father and the Holy Spirit,
ever one God, world without end. *Amen.*"

When, in addition, we keep in mind that
" THE SCRIPTURE CANNOT BE BROKEN,"* that
Christ has said, " Heaven and earth shall
pass away : but My words shall not pass away ;"†
and that the Scripture quoted by the Apostle
Peter says, " All flesh is as grass, and all the
glory of man as the flower of grass. The grass
withereth, and the flower thereof falleth away ;
but the word of the Lord endureth for ever.
And this is the word which by the Gospel is
preached unto you ;"‡ is it not beyond all controversy, that, according to the unalterable
Word of God, *the alone true* CHRIST has never
yet left heaven even once since His ascension
thither, and never will do so until His future
second advent ?

Therefore, whatever casuistical dust Romanists and Ritualists may throw in the eyes of

---

* John x. 35.   † Mark xiii. 31.   ‡ 1 Peter i. 24, 25.

their blinded dupes—however subtle, plausible, and bewildering may be the verbal conjuring, the confident assertions, and the tone of despotic authority used by them, they *cannot ever* have brought down, and they *never will* be able to bring down, the *true* Body and Blood of the *alone true* Christ of Holy Scripture to any altar or locality whatsoever on this earth. THEIR SHRINES ARE EMPTY SHRINES. Their " Christs " must be " FALSE CHRISTS,"* manufactured spiritually, metaphysically, and with the aid of wrongly applied texts of Scripture separated from their contexts ; and all this by imaginary " sacrificing " and mediatorial " priests," neither Jewish nor Christian, and, therefore, of corrupt creature origin.†

No distance interferes with the ceaseless and

* Matt. xxiv. 4, 21-31.

† Not Jewish. For after the atonement and ascension of Christ, He became the only High Priest of the Christian Church. The Aaronic Priesthood " were many priests," and " not suffered to continue by reason of death." But Christ, because " He continueth for ever, hath an unchangeable priesthood." The Aaronic priesthood, with its ceremonial types and shadows, was abolished (Heb. ix., x.).

Not Christian. For Christ's peculiar and mysterious type, " *without descent,*" was, like Christ, His antitype—UNIQUE. Christ concentrates all vicarious and mediatorial offices and prerogatives *in* HIMSELF ALONE (Heb. vii., ix., x). He is exclusively our PRIEST, ALTAR, and SACRIFICE, and His ever effectual intercession is carried on for those who believe in Him, *not on* EARTH, *but " in* HEAVEN itself" (Heb. i. 3, iv. 14-16, vi. 19-20, vii. 25-28, ix. 24-26 ; Rom. viii. 34).

active sympathy of the glorious Head of His true
and living Church—the "blessed company of
all faithful people," as defined in the Church of
England's Prayer Book. Are we not expressly
told that with that love of His "which passeth
knowledge," our perfect Mediator stooped to
our human necessities ? "For we have not an
High Priest which cannot be touched with the
feeling of our infirmities ; but was in all points
tempted like as we are, yet without sin. Let
us therefore come boldly unto the throne of
grace, that we may obtain mercy, and find grace
to help in time of need " (Heb. iv. 14-16, vii.
22-28). Has He not, in all ages, interposed on
behalf of His believing people, and comforted,
healed, soothed, led, and sustained them in all
their sorrows, troubles, dangers, sufferings, and
trials ? Has not the Lord Jesus expressly
taught us that, during His absence from them,
His people ought to honour Him and His written
Word by carrying out what He so frequently
emphasized and what His inspired Apostle
repeats, namely, "a walking by faith, and not
by sight " ? (2 Cor. v. 7). Did He not say to His
doubting disciple, "Thomas, because thou hast
seen Me, thou hast believed ; blessed are they

that have not seen, and yet have believed"? Does not the Apostle Peter, when alluding to the full realization of "salvation ready to be revealed in the last time," describe believers as "greatly rejoicing, though now for a season, if need be," as he adds, "·ye are in heaviness through manifold temptations: that the trial of your faith, being much more precious than of gold that perisheth, though it be tried with fire, might be found unto praise and honour and glory at the appearing of Jesus Christ: whom having not seen, ye love; in whom, though now ye see Him not, yet believing, ye rejoice with joy unspeakable and full of glory: receiving the end of your faith, even the salvation of your souls"? (1 Peter i. 5-9).

Meanwhile, is not the abiding sympathy of Christ for His tried and persecuted people expressed in those memorable words sent from heaven to arrest the mad career of that raging persecutor, Saul, "Saul, Saul, why persecutest thou ME?" (Acts ix. 1-6).

Nor can distance prevent our communion with Christ in heaven. If distances are nullified for our words through space, by the discovery given to man of the electric telegraph

and the telephone, what is that but a type of
the still greater marvels of the instantaneous,
upward flashing of the believer's prayers, inter-
cessions, and praises, by the spiritual wire, so
to speak, of FAITH ?   Moreover, if true love is
united to implicit trust in a faithful and un-
changing friend, and nourishes the heart with
affectionate memories and influences, causing
practical proofs that such friends love not only
" in word, neither in tongue ; but in deed, and
in truth " (1 John iii. 18), ought it not to be
unspeakably more so as regards the loving
feeding of our hearts on Christ, not alone in
the Lord's Supper, nor of necessity supremely
there, which no Scripture asserts—but habitually, and all day long ?

On this point one of the very ablest of witnesses against Tractarianism thus wrote :—
" That Christ is really present in the Eucharist,
who disputes ?   He is present where two or
three are gathered together in His name.   Were
this all that is meant by real presence, there
would be no need of some of the most extraordinary subtleties of Number Ninety.   The
question is whether Christ is corporally present
—*whether He is, in any sense, present in the*

Eucharist, as He is not in other ordinances. . . . .
To suppose the elements any way connected,
save as types and emblems, with Christ's body
—to talk of a real presence, local or 'super-
local,' simple or 'mysterious,' *is not only
needless, but an offence to truth—a snare
for souls.* The same as to the alleged
change in the elements. They are not
changed : why should they be ? — they
are but a sign—eating and drinking them
but a sign : 'It is the Spirit that quickeneth ;'
and the Spirit that is quickened. The quicken-
ing of *a spirit* must be by *a spiritual act.* Does
any one say, 'Then the elements may be dispensed
with ?' I answer no. The sign is Christ's appointment, and its use is obvious. It shows
forth Christ's death.* It shows forth what we

---

*1 Cor. xi. 26.—In addition to Mr. Young's remarks above. it is
interesting to know that old writers have observed that the Lord's
Supper is, in effect, A PREACHING OF THE GOSPEL. Matthew Henry,
commenting on the Apostle's remonstrance, "O foolish Galatians,
who hath bewitched you, that you should not obey the truth, before
whose eyes Jesus Christ hath been evidently set forth, crucified among
you," says, "Jesus Christ had been evidently set forth as crucified
among them ; that is, they had had the doctrine of the Cross preached
to them and the sacrament of the Lord's Supper administered among
them, in both which Christ crucified had been set before them. Now,
it was the greatest madness that could be for them, who had acquaint-
ance with such sacred mysteries and admittance to such great solem-
nities, not to obey the truth which was thus published to them and
signed and sealed in that ordinance."

derive from that death.   It shows forth our one-
ness with Him and with His Church.   *It shows
it forth*, it does not *make* it.   Its use is but the
occasion of realizing the thing signified.   This
realization is no more a *mere intellectual* than it
is a *bodily* act.   It is a pure act of faith—a discerning the Lord's body, and feeding upon it—
discerning it where it is, *not in the bread and
wine, but where Stephen saw it, at God's right
hand*,* feeding on it as a spirit must feed on
what is substantial, not by eating and drinking,
but by a spiritual faculty.   There is nothing in
all this peculiar to the Eucharist, so as to make
it, as Tractarians make it, *the* feeding on Christ.
*Faith does it habitually : it is her vital act, like
breathing.*   But as all our faculties find special
occasions, so this ordinance is an appointed time,
with appointed means and encouragements, for
faith to act.   This is the only sound view of the

---

* In Foxe's " Book of Martyrs " it is related that when the Lady Anne
Askew was tormented with questionings by her Popish persecutors,
especially as to whether or not she believed that the true body and
blood of Christ was contained in the pyx, she asked them *why
Stephen was martyred by the Jewish priests.*   Seeing the force of her
question, and that they would have to answer that it was because
Stephen asserted that he had seen " the Son of Man standing on
the right hand of God" in heaven (Acts vii. 55-60), they declined to
answer.   Was not that proceeding a striking parallel to the way in
which the Jewish priests treated our Lord's question ? (Mark xi. 27-33).

Sacrament. It agrees with the whole analogy of Scripture truth, and with every syllable of the Liturgy of our truly Scriptural Church. . . . . The whole virtue of the Sacrament is in the beautiful direction, ' *Feed on Him in thy heart by faith with thanksgiving.*' To this feeding on Christ, *the actual absence or presence of Christ's body are, as we have seen, indifferent.*"*

" Christ," as Dean Close preached, "dwells not in bread and wine, but in the souls of His penitent, believing people, and that not merely ' sacramentally,' or 'ineffably,' or after some strange, mystical method in which He must be supposed to inhabit wheaten bread or ' the fruit of the wine,' but actually, plainly, spiritually, ' we dwell in Christ and Christ in us, we are one with Christ and Christ with us ; ' *by a union not confined to this Holy Sacrament*, though there enjoyed in the highest degree, but according to His most true promise, " Where two or three are met together in My name, there am I in the midst of them;' *there* is a REAL PRESENCE; and, individually, ' If a man love Me, he will keep My words : and My Father will love him,

---

* " Protestantism or Popery," by the Rev. Edward Young, M.A. (2nd ed., Nisbet & Co., 1843).

and WE will come unto him, and make Our abode
with him ' (John xiv. 23), not sacramentally, for
nothing is here spoken of a sacrament, but by
that indwelling Spirit by which He lives and
walks in His people."*

"*Feed on Him in thy heart by faith with
thanksgiving.*" Can such feeding on Christ
be separated from *any* appointed Scripture
means of grace? *Without* it, can there be
any true prayer, or praise, in our private devo-
tions, our family worship, or our public worship?
Does Holy Scripture anywhere promise any
special or particular grace in connection with
the Lord's Supper that is not equally and,
indeed, more definitely promised in connection
with believing prayer, the preached Gospel, the
study of the Bible, or sanctified affliction? If
so, *where* does the Word of God so teach?
That the Lord's Supper ought to be a specially
heart-affecting occasion, and one especially to
stir up the forgiven and saved believer's godly
sorrow, gratitude, and praise, to deepen our love
to Christ, and to increase our brotherly affection
for all true believers, is another matter.

* "Our Absent Lord, not present in the Sacramental Elements."
Sermon preached in substance in Carlisle Cathedral on Ascension Day,
1867, by Francis Close, D.D., Dean of Carlisle. (Hatchard, 1867.)

Some persons refer us to 1 Cor. x. 16 :— "The cup of blessing which we bless, is it not the communion of the blood of Christ? The bread which we break, is it not the communion of the body of Christ?"

But laying the stress on the verb and word " IS," as though it did not plainly mean *represents*, as in "I am the true Vine," "I am the Door," &c., they *overlook the context*, in which we find the same verb similarly used in vers. 4, 17, as in ver. 16, and where it *must* mean "represents," as many of our great divines have pointed out in replying to Romanists. The Apostle, alluding to Christ's believing Israel, *before* the Incarnation of Christ, and *before* the institution of the Lord's Supper, says they "did all eat *the* SAME spiritual meat, and did all drink the *same* spiritual drink, for they drank of that spiritual Rock that followed them; and that Rock WAS Christ" (vers. 1-4). Now, if the word "*is*" in ver. 16 be taken *literally*, then must the word "*was*" be also taken literally, unless Holy Scripture be inconsistently interpreted in favour of special pleading.

Besides, as has been shown by the Rev. Dr.

M

John Harrison, in his learned " Reply to Dr. Pusey's Challenge," and by Dean Goode, in his work on the Eucharist, " the body of Christ," in ver. 16, is connected with " the one head and one body " in ver. 17, and with the same Apostle's declaration, " Now YE ARE the body of Christ," in 1 Cor. x. 11, 27.

The " Monthly Letter of the Protestant Alliance " for July, 1889, contains much valuable matter on " Rome's Sacramental System." Part of it is here given, with a hope that the reader will refer to the Letter.

" The Church of Rome affirms that, in the Mass, the so-called priest offers up a propitiatory sacrifice for the remission of sins. She therefore wields an influence of immense power over the minds and souls of her subjects. Men who believe that she has this power are her willing slaves, for once a man is firmly persuaded that a priest, by his mediation, can procure forgiveness of his sins, and obtain mitigation of eternal punishment for him, he will gladly give to that priest all that he requires, to the utmost farthing, in order to secure for himself such an inestimable blessing. The Romanizing teaching of the Ritualistic clergy on this point leads on to this fatal belief in Romish doctrines. It enhances the office of the priest, declares the need of *continued* sacrifice, detracts from the finished work of Christ, and ignores the power of the One Mediator.

" 3066. TRANSUBSTANTIATION.—It is therefore of importance briefly to expose the fallacy of the Romish Sacramental System. The subject has been exhaustively handled in Elliott's 'Delineation of Romanism,' published by the Wesleyan Conference, and in several valuable works ; but, to many, it is difficult to peruse a lengthened dissertation, and therefore it is desirable to offer a refutation of the doctrine of Transubstantiation in the shorter and more accessible form presented by the ' Monthly Letter.'*

"The doctrine of Transubstantiation is strictly defined by the Decrees of the Council of Trent, and in the Catechism of the Council of Trent authoritatively explained. These authoritative definitions establish the following points :—

"(1.) That by virtue of the words of Consecration, *Hoc est enim Corpus meum*, there is neither bread nor wine left on the table.

---

* For a fuller treatment of this subject, the reader is referred to Elliott's work, from which the statements made in the " Monthly Letter " have been chiefly compiled.

"3068. The Words of Consecration.— Romish theologians argue that by the words, 'This is My body,' Christ consecrated and transubstantiated the elements of bread and wine; but may not the words of 'blessing' or the 'giving of thanks,' with equal reason, be held to be the words of consecration?

"Is it not the more natural interpretation to believe that our Saviour meant the disciples to understand that the bread which they were eating *represented* His body, which in the course of a few hours was to be crucified? It is an ordinary figure of speech to point to a picture and say, ' This is the Queen ;' or to take a map of England and say of a particular place, ' This is London,' using the term ' This is,' for ' This represents,' or ' This signifies.' In the Scriptures we find constant use of such language. Thus, ' The seven kine *are* (that is *represent*) seven years' (Gen. xli. 26). ' Judah *is* a lion's whelp' (Gen. xlix. 9). ' This is the bread of affliction which our fathers ate in the land of Egypt.' ' Thy word *is* a lamp to my feet' (Ps. cxviii. 105). ' The ten horns are ten kings' (Dan. vii. 24). ' That rock was (that is *represented*) Christ' (1 Cor. x. 4). ' The seven stars are the angels of the seven churches, and the seven candlesticks are (that is *represent*) the seven churches' (Rev. i. 20). Our Saviour also says 'I *am* the Vine—I am the Door—I am the Shepherd,' evidently using those terms in a figurative sense.

"3069. THE RITUAL OF THE PASSOVER.— Similar language was used at the observance of the Passover. It was directed that when the children of the Israelites, then present, should ask 'the meaning of this service,' the Elders were directed to explain the reasons for the feast, and to say, 'It is the sacrifice of the Lord's Passover.' (Exod. xii. 26, 27).

"The learned Jewish commentator, Maimonides Pesach, has fully described the ceremonial used at the observance of the Passover, a ceremonial which is strikingly in accordance with the Mosaic teaching. Maimonides relates that at this feast four cups of wine were drunk, that the table was furnished with the pascal lamb, bitter herbs, two cakes of unleavened bread, and a thick sauce made of dates, figs, raisins, vinegar, &c., mingled together, to *represent* the clay of which their ancestors made bricks in Egypt."*

" From the foregoing it would appear that the Last Supper was conducted in accordance with the Jewish Ceremonial observed at the Feast of the Passover, and that our Lord followed out to the letter the Mosaic instructions, saying to the Disciples, ' This is (that is *represents*) the Lord's Passover.' In accordance with the directions given in Exodus xii. 26, 27, our Lord, doubtlessly, proceeded to explain that these ceremonies were observed as a *remembrance* of the deliverance of the Children of Israel from bondage in Egypt, and of God's mercy in sparing the Israelites when He smote the Egyptians. Following up this train of reasoning, we can see how suitable it was that, after supper, our Lord should give a name to the last cup that was drunk and to the last piece of bread that was eaten, and, in similar language to that used in reference to the other symbols consumed at the feast, should say, ' This is (that is *represents*) My body broken and given

---

* See Elsley's " Annotations on the Four Gospels " (Oxford, 1844), p. 228, on St. Matt. c. 26. Also Bishop Lightfoot's "Temple Service," xiii. 1.

for you,' and 'This cup of wine is (that is
represents) My blood, which is shed for many for
the remission of sins.' 'Do this in *remembrance* of Me.'"

Our blessed Lord has very solemnly warned
us against FALSE CHRISTS (Matt. xxiv. 24-26),
and to guard us against "false Christs, and
false prophets, [who] shall show great signs and
wonders; insomuch that, if it were possible,
they shall deceive the very elect,"* He subjoins
a description of His appearance and the accom
panying circumstances, which will certify the
real presence with which He THE TRUE CHRIST
will manifest His next appearance to the inhabitants of our earth. *In that sublime and awful
light, what becomes of the mock pretences and
theatrical display of the Mass priests and*

---

* And, on our Lord's additional warning, "Wherefore if they
shall say unto you, Behold, he is in the desert, go not forth: Behold,
he is in the secret chambers, believe it not," Archbishop USHER
points out how applicable it is to the blasphemous as well as
absurd claim of the Church of Rome, in connection with her
Mass wafer, to "*keep under lock and key*" in their pyxes Christ's *Deity*,
which "the heaven and heaven of heavens cannot contain" (3 Kings
viii. 27), and also His *Humanity*, which being, as allowed by the
Church of Rome, to be in heaven, cannot also be on earth and in
millions of wafers. See the exhaustive historical treatise on "The
Real Presence" heresy, and its resultant Transubstantiation, in the
Archbishop's "Answer to a Jesuit." He mentions some most astounding "lying wonders," alleged to have occurred in connection with the
host.

Eucharistic Ritualists and their performances?
(Compare with vers. 29-42, Daniel vii. 9-14 ;
2 Thess. i. 4-12, ii. 8 ; Rev. xix. 11-21 ; Zech.
xiv. 1-9).

Now, "false CHRISTS" require false APOSTLES,
and *simulated Christian teaching*, or *a measure
of Gospel truth* mixed up with doctrines, which
—as Hooker points out, "*by consequent,*"
but not "directly" * —subtly "overturn the
foundation" of the Christian faith.   Otherwise
how could our Lord and Master's warning be
verified, that, the "false Christs" would be
able to deceive multitudes, and, "if it were
possible"—which, blessed be our God, it is *not*
—to "deceive the very elect"?

So, we also have in the Word of God a
merciful warning against "false apostles" of
the most ensnaring kind.   The Apostle Paul
alludes to the beguilement of Eve by Satan
coming *not as an Infidel, not denying God's
Word*, but *suggesting false meanings in it ;* not
saying plainly, "Ye shall *not* die," but "Ye shall
not *surely* die."   Thus infusing scepticism, just as
in our days clergymen and moral men are doing.
The Apostle emphatically warns the Corinthian

---

* On Justification.

Christians against the same evil angel, expressing his fears " lest by any means, as the serpent
beguiled Eve through his subtlety, so their minds
should be corrupted from the simplicity that is
in Christ."

Yes, " corrupted from the *simplicity* that is
in Christ," into the *complexity* even then at
work introductory to the labyrinthine system of
ANTICHRIST, or the CHURCH OF ROME.

No open Infidel, no open Socinian, as Bishop
Christopher Wordsworth, as Hooker, and other
learned men have pointed out, could possibly
come near to "deceiving the very elect."

The Apostle thus describes the TRANS-
FORMERS OF OTHERS and themselves as kaleido-
scopic CHAMELEONS. "Such," he says, "are false
apostles, deceitful workers, transforming themselves into the Apostles of Christ. And no
marvel, for Satan himself is transformed into an
angel of light. Therefore it is no great thing
if his ministers also be transformed as the
ministers of righteousness, whose end shall be
according to their works" (2 Cor. xi. 1-3, 13-
15). Nor is this all. For after Christ's
resurrection, we find Him expressing His
approval of the angel of the Church of Ephesus,

saying, " I know thy works, and thy labour,
and thy patience, and how thou canst not bear
them which are evil : and thou hast tried them
which say they are apostles, and are not, and
hast found them liars " (Rev. ii. 1, 2).

Now, ought not such Scriptures to lead wise
and thoughtful men to look *with special fear
and inquiry* on any professing Christian Church,
or clergy, claiming exclusive APOSTOLIC prerogatives, power, and authority ? Should not their
doctrines and practices be most carefully tested
by Holy Scripture ? Particularly if they are
found eclipsing its light, and, whilst not denying the Word of God, yet "*making it of none
effect* by their traditions" and subverting
glosses, whilst forbidding their flocks to read
the Word of God for themselves, *without
explanatory and obligatory notes or comments
cleverly supplied by what is erroneously called
the* CHURCH ?

Is not such salutary caution increased when
we find another prophetic warning of the utmost
consequence—as history has shown—stating
that THE APOSTASY from the Christian Faith to
be revealed in what is known as Christendom was
symbolized by A FALSE APOSTLE ? For the title

" Son of Perdition " used by the Apostle is the
very name applied by our Lord to Judas (John
xvii. 12).

Moreover, as Judas is said by our Lord to be,
whilst *a professed Apostle*, yet all the while " a
devil " (John vi. 66-71), is it not most impressive
that, *externally*, he was so like a true Apostle,
that when, at the last Passover Supper, our
Lord profoundly alarmed His Apostles by the
startling announcement, "Verily I say unto you,
that one of you shall betray Me," so far were the
eleven from suspecting Judas, that with deep
humility, and in the spirit of our martyr, John
Bradford, who, seeing a criminal led to execution
feelingly said, " *But for the grace of God, there
goes John Bradford,*" " they were exceeding
sorrowful, and began every one to say unto Him,
Lord, is it I " ?

Moreover, amongst other typical marks, Judas
was a covetous man, who, whilst he " kept the
bag " containing all the worldly wealth of our
Master and His Apostles, out of which he was
deputed to " give something to the poor" (John
xiii. 21-29), yet personally " he cared not for the
poor " (John xii. 1-6); and angry apparently at
losing the proceeds of the " ointment," he went

off and "covenanted with the chief priests and captains how he might betray Him unto them," and *those priestly murderers by proxy* covenanted to give him thirty pieces of silver" (Zech. xi. 10-17), the price of *a slave*, for Him who, at a priceless cost, come to set poor lost sinners free !

The Church of Rome is especially marked by what in France is called "*La religion d'argent,*" "the religion of money." Her children are taught all their lifetime to endeavour to purchase, by works and money paid to the priests for Masses and on other accounts, what God offers, for Christ's sake, as a "*free gift*" (Rom. v. 8-19, vi. 15-23; 1 Peter i. 8-25). In vain do they earnestly and piously labour to fill a bottomless tub with water, or to roll a classic wheel up a hill, only to find it returning on them. True peace of conscience, and true peace of mind, in the prospect of death and the Judgment Day, by such a system are impossibilities. It is prophesied of the APOSTASY that the woman would "make merchandise of the souls of men," besides other of her features in Rev. xviii. 12, 13.

One point calls for careful attention. As Bishop Wordsworth points out, no "*Mystery* of

Iniquity " can be accomplished by either an *open Infidel* or an *open Socinian*. Moreover, we find in the New Testament *germs* whose developments essentially fit the Church of Rome. For instance, *Mariolatry* and a strife for the Primacy (Matt. xii. 46-49 ; Mark iii. 31-35 ; Matt. xx. 20-29), *Apostolical Succession* and *Intolerance* (Mark ix. 33-42).

One thing is sure. The ANTICHRIST to be " *destroyed* " at Christ's coming, having first been " *consumed*," *did already work when the Apostle wrote his epistle*. Eighteen centuries have elapsed since that date. Evidently that prophecy cannot possibly apply to any single individual man.*

What are the doctrines of the Church of Rome, in her own words, respecting her MASS ?

Does she, or does she not, in connection with it, however unwittingly, herself bear witness to the appalling fulfilment by her Popes and priesthood of the momentous prophecy concerning " the man of sin, the son of perdition : he that

---

* So far as the writer is aware, no answer rebutting the facts and arguments in the late Rev. Professor T. R. Birks' two volumes on " Elements of Prophecy " and " The First Two Visions of Daniel," exposing the errors of the FUTURIST School of Prophecy, has yet appeared. They are quoted with approval in Mr. Grattan Guinness's widely known work, " The Approaching End of the Age."

opposeth and exalteth himself against all that
is called God, or that is worshipped so that he
sitteth in the temple [margin " sanctuary "]
of God, *setting himself forth as* GOD "? (2 Thess.
ii. 3-4, R.V.).

Bishop Christopher Wordsworth thus renders
the passage, giving in a note his important
explanation of the word " temple " (See his
" Union with Rome," p. 52).

"*Then*, says the Apostle, *shall the Man of Sin*,
or that Lawless One (ὁ ἄνομος), *be revealed, the
Son of Perdition, who opposeth and exalteth
himself above all that is called God, or that
is worshipped, so that he, as God, sitteth in the*
TEMPLE *of* GOD, *showing himself that he is God.**

"The words here rendered *so that he sitteth in
the Temple of God* (καθίσαι εἰς ναὸν) are remarkable. Nαὸς, the word rendered *Temple*, is the
holier part of the Temple,—the *Sanctuary*, where
the ALTAR *is ;* and καθίσαι εἰς ναὸν are words in-
volving *motion*, and signify to be conveyed or to
convey himself and take a seat in the *Holy
Place* of the Temple of God, or the Christian
Church."†

---

* 2 Thess. ii. 3, 4.

† There are about twenty-five passages in the Acts of the Apostles,
where the Jewish Temple is called ἱερὸν, but not a single one where it is

For the limited purposes contemplated in these pages, the following extracts will, it is thought, be found sufficient. For convenience of reference they are here marked A. B. C.

A.

QUESTION XXVI.

. . . . " The true body of Christ the Lord, the very same that was born of the Virgin, and sits at the right hand of the Father in heaven, is contained in this sacrament ; the second, that, however alien to, and remote from, the senses it may seem, no substance of the elements remains therein." . . . .

B.

QUESTION LXXIV.

"We, therefore, confess that the sacrifice of the Mass is and ought to be considered one and the same as that of the cross, as the Victim is one and the same, namely, Christ our Lord, who

---

called ναὸς, nor is there one, in any of the Apostolic Epistles, where it bears this name. The ναὸς τοῦ Θεοῦ, in the mouth of an Apostle speaking to *Gentile* Christians concerning the *future*, cannot mean the *Jewish* Temple, and can only mean the *Christian Church*. Compare Macknight's note on this passage (2 Thess. ii. 2, 3) : " The sitting of the Man of Sin in the *Temple of God*, signifies his being a *Christian by profession*, and that he would exercise his usurped authority in the *Christian Church*."

immolated Himself once only, after a bloody
manner, on the altar of the Cross. For the
bloody and unbloody Victim are not two victims, but one only, whose sacrifice is daily re-
newed in the Eucharist, in obedience to the
command of the Lord: 'Do this for a com-
memoration of Me.'"

C.

QUESTION LXXV.

" But the priest also is one and the same Christ
the Lord ; for the ministers who offer sacrifice,
when they consecrate His body and blood, act
not in their own, but in the person of Christ, as
is shown by the words of consecration itself; for
the priest does not say, 'This is the body of
Christ,' but 'This is My body;' and thus representing Christ the Lord, he changes the substance of the bread and wine into the true substance of His body and blood."

D.

QUESTION XXXV.

. . . . "If, after consecration, the body of
Christ is really and truly under the species of
bread and wine, not having been there before,
it must have become so by change of place, by

creation, or by the change of another thing into it. But that the body of Christ cannot be in the sacrament by change of place is evident, as it would then cease to be in heaven, for whatever is moved must necessarily cease to occupy the place from which it is moved. Still less can we suppose that the body of Christ is rendered present by creation, an idea which cannot even be conceived in thought. It remains, therefore, that the body of our Lord be in the sacrament, because the bread is changed into it, and, therefore, it necessarily follows that no substance of the bread remains."*

It will be seen, that, according to extract A, it is allowed by the Church of Rome that— " The *true* body of Christ the Lord, *the very same that was born of the Virgin, sits at the right hand of the Father in heaven.*"

Nevertheless, as she assents, that *same* body of Christ is *also* " contained in this sacrament " of the Mass.

Further, that, although chemical and other tests prove beyond doubt that the " conse-

---

* Catechism of the Council of Trent. Translated into English, with Notes, &c., by Very Rev. J. Donovan, D.D., E. Professor, Maynooth College, &c., &c. (Dublin : James Duffy.)

crated " bread remains bread, and will surely
see " corruption," which Christ's *true* body could
not experience (Acts ii. 22-32), yet, " however
alien to, and remote from the senses it may
seem, no substance of the elements [of bread
and wine] remains therein." In other words,
only an *appearance* of bread, or of wine,
remains.

In extract D, the Church of Rome explains
how, after admitting that, " the true body of
Christ, the very same that was born of the
Virgin," *still* " *sits* at the right hand of the
Father in heaven," she yet manages, by the use
of the magical and stupendously miraculous
words, " this is My body," pronounced by one
of her priests, to provide a *different* and yet also
a body *identical* with Christ's true body in
heaven. So that two are one, and one is two.

" *If*"—she says more correctly perhaps than
intended, yet, as not a few plain men who shun
casuistry and theological transformations will
think, most appropriately—" If, after consecration, the body of Christ is really and truly under
the species of bread and wine," then :—

(*a.*) It cannot be there " by change of place,"
and yet is there, and can be carried about from

place to place by her priests, and can by them be located in millions of wafers, in millions of places on the earth. Yet, all the while, it *cannot* "cease to be in heaven."

(*b.*) "Still less," she says, "can we suppose that the body of Christ is rendered present by creation." Yet what are their priestly acts but claims verbally to make God ?

But was not "the *true* body of Christ" originally rendered present "by creation"? Does not the Church of Rome herself say of that "*true* body of Christ," that it " *was born of the Virgin* "? Does not the Athanasian Creed Scripturally teach that our Lord Jesus Christ is " God, of the substance of the Father, · begotten before the worlds : and Man, of the substance of his Mother, born in the world. Perfect God, and perfect Man : of a reasonable soul and human flesh subsisting. Equal to the Father, as touching His Godhead : and inferior to the Father, as touching His manhood"? If that be so, what are we to think of *that* " body of Christ " said by the Church of Rome to be introduced by her priests "under the species of bread and wine," but which is *not* "created " ?

(c.) "It remains, therefore," says the Church
of Rome, "that the body of our Lord
be in the sacrament, *because the bread is
changed into it*, and, therefore, it necessarily
follows" [so, at least, argues the Church of
Rome] "that no substance of the bread
remains."

Now, since according to Holy Scripture, to
the Athanasian Creed, and to the statement of
the Church of Rome herself, the *true* body of
Christ was taken from " the substance of His
Mother," the Virgin Mary, is it *a fact* that the
Virgin Mary's substance was formed " *of bread
changed into it* "? If it *was* so formed, which
not even the Church of Rome would probably
so *de-naturalize*, and so dishonour the Virgin
Mary by asserting—how could her body be that
of *a true and natural human being and a
descendant of Eve* "? But, if the Virgin's
substance was *not* so formed, what must we
think of that *other* " body of our Lord " said by
the Church of Rome to be " in the sacrament "?
Can two essentially different bodies be yet one
and the same body? Can two bodies formed
out of totally different substances be, nevertheless, regarded as identical?

We hear a good deal of the shifts and contrivances, not alone of Romanists, but also of
their facsimiles in Tractarians and Ritualists, of
a sort of Christ of their own invention, who is
said to be really present on earth, *before the
time which God has appointed*, and who appears
in chancels and on altars "after a spiritual
manner," or "after the manner of a spirit"
flatly contradicting Scripture (Luke xxiv. 36-
42). This Christ is said to be present in some
" ineffable " and *super*-natural way, which,
therefore, must needs be a "*non*-natural" way.
Dr. Pusey and others have asserted, without
the shadow of a proof from Holy Scripture, that
Christ GOD-MAN passed *through the substance*
of the doors which "were shut when the
disciples were assembled for fear of the Jews"
(John xx. 19).

Now, if that had been the case, it would
follow that our Lord's resurrection with the
same body that He had before His death could
not be proved. But He invited His disciples *to
test His identity*, not only by *seeing* Him, but
also by *handling* Him, by seeing Him eat, and by
encouraging doubting Thomas to apply his
finger to the scars that He bore. *True* " flesh

and bones " such as He had, as " perfect Man,"
could not, according to the laws of nature
ordained of God, have passed through the wood.
Why needed it to do so ?   Was not Peter
imprisoned between two soldiers, to whom he
was " bound with two chains."   Were not the
lives of " the keepers " of the prison sure to be
forfeited, as indeed happened, if he escaped ?
(Acts xii. 1-10, 19).   Yet an angel delivered
him from his chains, and " *the iron gate opened
of itself*" to let Peter escape.   Why, then,
might not the Lord cause the door of the room
where the disciples were to *open of itself?*
Moreover, are we not told that when " Jesus
drew near " to the two disciples going to
Emmaus, " their eyes were holden, that they
should not know Him " ? (Luke xxiv. 13-16).

Romanists and others tell us of the mysterious qualities of Christ's " glorified body."
That CHRIST HIMSELF was glorified at His
ascension into heaven—that His scarred but
incorruptible resurrection body was then
gloriously honoured, and that we read in Psalm
xxiv. 7-10 of the triumphant display of His
glorious victory over death, Satan, and the
grave, and in the Apocalypse of a manifestation

"in the midst of the throne" of "a lamb as it had been slain" (Rev. v. 6)— all that is revealed to us. But where are we told in Scripture that Christ needed, *like us*, a changed body—a body different from the one with which He walked on the surface of the lake as on the land, and with which, as "*that* SAME Jesus," He majestically ascended up to heaven ?

Bishop Jewel, replying to the Jesuit, Harding, says, "But to what end allegeth M. Harding the spiritual state of Christ's glorious body? Doth he not remember that the old heretic Abbot Eutychus maintained his fantasies by the same, and was deceived ? *Christ's body,* said he, *is glorious : Therefore it is changed into the very substance and nature of God, and hath now no shape or proportion of a body.* This is an old heresie" (Reply, Article 5, Dio. 7).

Dean Goode* cites our great Bishop in a striking passage here abbreviated :—" Over all this M. Harding throweth a sweet mist, to carry away the simple in the dark : Christ's body, saith he, is in the Sacrament, not by

---

* On the Eucharist.

local, but by substantial presence ; carnally,
but not in carnal manner ; placed in the pix, in
the hand, in the mouth, and yet in no place at
all. . . . There now where before it was not,
and yet without any shifting or change of place."
[This is an accurate description of our authors,
as fully described by Archdeacon Wilberforce.]
UNLESS THIS MAN WERE FAST ASLEEP, HE COULD
NEVER FALL INTO SO DEEP A DREAM. In these
fantasies he seemeth well to agree with the old
heretics. For even such a body they imagined
that Christ received of the blessed Virgin ; and
yet were they heretics notwithstanding. For,
which of all the old learned Fathers ever
taught us this strange doctrine ? Who ever
durst so spoil Christ of His place, of His quan-
tity, and of the natural proportions of His
body ? . . . . M. Harding, to maintain his
errors, and to avoid infinite absurdities, is
driven to say, There are *two Christs*, the one
local, the other not local ; the one above, the
other beneath ; the one with proportion of
body, the other without proportion. . . . . In
ten thousand places Christ's body is full and
whole ; and yet all these are but one body.
Thus, *one is many, and many are one; above is*

beneath, and beneath is above; local is not local, and not local is local ; and all this without the authority either of God's holy Word, or of any one old Catholic Father. These be M. Harding's Catholic conclusions ; *even the very same* that were used and avouched by Eutychus, Apollinarius, Manichæans, and other like heretics in old times."*

Now, there is and there can be · but ONE ORIGINAL of any person or thing whatsoever— any amount of facsimiles, copies, likenesses statues, architectural or other carvings, but ONLY ONE TRUE ORIGINAL. Therefore, there is only ONE Triune God, only ONE true Christ God-

* Reply to Harding's Answer (Art. 6, Works Parker Society ed., vol. i., pp. 484, 485). Dean Goode, in his important work on the Eucharist, shows that the doctrines so powerfully traversed by Bishop Jewel are, in all essential features, precisely those taught by Dr. Pusey, Archdeacon Wilberforce, and others of that Romish school. *A "spiritual* manner " of Christ's appearing is not *the true* manner of His appearing either before or after His death and resurrection.   For He *ever had and He ever will have in His "incorruptible" body "* flesh and bones " which can be " seen " and " handled."   Hence, witnessing apparently against *the transforming Gnostics,* in and by whom some of the elements of the " Mystery of Iniquity " were already working (2 Thess. ii. 7-10), the beloved Apostle expressly witnesses, as he says, to " That which was from the beginning, which we have heard, which we have seen with our eyes, which we have looked upon, and our hands have handled, of the word of life " (1 John i. 1).   Possibly, with or without the aid of " SPIRITUALISTS " and evil spirits, Romanists or Ritualists may work MIGHTY " SIGNS AND WONDERS," RIVALLING GOD'S TRUE MIRACLES.   What then ?   Are we not expressly warned in God's holy Word *against that very contingency,*

Man, who is *the* Prophet, *the* Priest, *the* all-atoning Sacrifice for the sins of the whole world, and *the* one Mediator and Intercessor for us with God. In each and in all of those offices, Christ's prerogatives and their blessings ARE ABSOLUTELY UNSHAREABLE.

Only one original! If so, then, what must be the character of the reputed Christs in millions, claimed and exhibited by the Romish and Ritualistic priests? What can they have all along been? what can they be other than *mock originals;* in other words, the " FALSE CHRIST'S," against which we are so emphatically warned in Holy Scripture?

lighted up afresh to some extent by the warnings both in Rev. xvi. 15-21, and 2 Thess. ii. 7-17 ; 2 Cor. iv. 1-6, xi. 1-15 ? Are we not told that such "sign or wonder," to confirm the *false claims, false powers,* and *false prerogatives* of " false apostles," may actually "come to pass," and may be allowed ? Why ? " For the Lord your God proveth you, to know whether ye love the Lord your God with all your heart and with all your soul. Ye shall walk after the Lord your God, and fear Him, and keep His commandments, and obey His voice, and ye shall serve Him, and cleave to Him " (Deut. xiii. 1-4). Is there not a parallel warning in the New Testament, where we are told that "there must be heresies among you" [including—may we not suppose ?— *a separatist priestly caste* separating itself and others from Christ to human traditions and pagan practices] "that they which are approved may be made manifest among you." Is not the corollary *this,* namely, that *be the supernatural signs and wonders what they may, if they are employed in opposition to the sole prerogatives of Christ and to Gospel Truth,* we are to disregard them, and to remember our Saviour's charge, " Be thou faithful unto death, and I will give thee a crown of life " ? (Rev. ii. 2, 9-11).

But what of that most appalling manifestation of the Man of Sin and Son of Perdition,
"*setting himself forth as God*"? Never for one
moment must we forget that Christ is "perfect GOD as well as perfect MAN," or we shall
miss the deep meaning attaching to that phrase,
"The MYSTERY of INIQUITY." Will not the
actual words of the Church of Rome be read
with unspeakable awe and horror, as they are
set forth in extracts B and C?

First of all, we have to note that whereas
the Word of God declares that "*without
shedding of blood* is *no* remission of sins (Heb.
ix. 11-22), the Church of Rome exhibits *two
different* "victims" or sacrifices. One of these
is "bloody," or capable of shedding, *not simply
material blood*, but in reality his LIFE on behalf
of our forfeited lives. Thus we read, "Whoso
sheddeth man's blood, by man shall his blood
be shed," and in a previous verse we read,
"Flesh with the LIFE thereof, which is the
BLOOD thereof, shall ye not eat" (Gen. ix.
4, 6). This injunction is repeated in Lev.
iii. 17, xvii. 10-14, and elsewhere. Believers
are said to come to "Jesus, the Mediator of
the new covenant, and to the blood of sprinkling

that speaketh better things than that of Abel"
(Heb. xii. 22-25). Our blessed Saviour, with un-
utterable affection towards poor wandering per-
ishing sinners, and specially for His beloved
Bride, says, "I am the good Shepherd : the good
Shepherd giveth His life for the sheep."
"Therefore doth My Father love Me, because I lay
down My life that I might take it again. No
man taketh it from Me, but I lay it down of
Myself. I have power to lay it down, and I
have power to take it again. This commandment have I received of My Father" (John x.
14-18).

In another place that all important truth is
thus expressed : "Neither by the blood of goats
and calves, but by His own blood, He entered
in once into the holy place, having obtained
eternal redemption for us"* (Heb. ix. 8-24).

Thus the living Redeemer, the " PRINCE OF
LIFE," could lay down His inestimably precious
life for us.

---

* Dr. Adolph Saphir, in a beautiful Sermon on the Lord's Supper
from our Lord's words, "With desire I have desired to eat this Passover with you before I suffer " (Luke xxii. 15), preaching in the Scotch
Church, Bournemouth, on Nov. 2, 1890, remarked "that it was wonderful what a collection of precious Gospel gems our Lord had concentrated
in the simple, but profoundly significant rite of the commemorative
Supper." He beautifully said, "We are reminded of Christ *for* us, Christ

But what is that *other* sacrifice of the Church of Rome which she herself characterizes as " *un-bloody*," and, therefore, *without life*—a *dead* sacrifice only fit for the worship and the dark realms of the PRINCE OF DEATH ? Does it not answer to that " different Gospel, which is not another *Gospel*" (Gal. i. 8, 9, R.V.), preached by deceivers who " would pervert the Gospel of Christ, and against which the Apostle, with holy jealousy for the glory of God our Saviour, utters his anathema " ?

To what a climax have we now arrived ! Is it possible that men *of themselves* could have devised it ?

The *priest* of the Church of Rome who performs the MASS, does not do so *in remembrance of, nor in honour of Christ*, but actually *claims to be* CHRIST HIMSELF, that is, *claims, by a* " *Mystery of Iniquity*," to be GOD ! For Christ is " perfect God " and " perfect Man."

---

in us, Christ *with* us, and Christ *coming to us*." Christ the centre of history, Christ the light and the life of the Holy Scriptures. " It was not because Christ was the Great Teacher, not because of His sinless life, not because He was a perfect pattern of goodness and of all virtues, not because He was the Son of God, but emphatically, and in accordance with His prophetic office, which testified of Him that ' by His own blood ' He entered into heaven itself, now to appear in the presence of God for us."

Note carefully the Church of Rome's actual words :—

"The priest also IS ONE AND THE SAME CHRIST THE LORD."

Mark further the reason assigned for that fearfully blasphemous usurpation :—

"*For* the ministers who offer sacrifice, when they consecrate His body and blood, ACT NOT IN THEIR OWN, but IN THE PERSON OF CHRIST, as is shown by the words of consecration itself, *for the priest does not say,* ' This is the body of Christ,' but ' This is MY body ; and THUS REPRESENTING CHRIST THE LORD, he changes the substance of the bread and wine into the true substance of HIS body and blood."

Is any further proof needed to show, out of the Church of Rome's own mouth, that she has fulfilled that essential mark of the predicted APOSTASY and ANTICHRIST, of which it is said that he shall " SET HIMSELF FORTH AS GOD " ?

Is there not but too awful a justification for the faithful protest of the Protestant Churches against " the blasphemous fables and dangerous deceits " of the Mass ; and for the no less Scriptural and faithful witness of the Church of England's " Black Rubric," declaring that, to worship the supposed presence of Christ in, with, or under the bread and wine *consecrated* —that is, *set apart for a sacred purpose*, as churches and burial grounds are consecrated— " IS IDOLATRY TO BE ABHORRED OF EVERY FAITHFUL CHRISTIAN " ?

Is it not evident that, on their own showing, both Romanists and Ritualists, by claiming that *each* piece of the millions of pieces of bread contains their God and Saviour, involve themselves necessarily in the terrible guilt and idolatry of the *polytheistic* heathen, of whom the inspired Apostle says :—

" Though there be that are called gods, whether in heaven or on earth ; as there are gods many, and lords many ; yet to us there is one God, the Father, of whom are all things, and we unto Him ; and one Lord, Jesus Christ, through whom are all things, and we through Him " ? (1 Cor. viii. 5, 6, R.V.).

Are we not forcibly reminded of the Psalmist's words, only substituting " bread " for metals, where he says, " Their idols are silver and gold, the work of men's hands. . . . . They that make them are like unto them ; so is every one that trusteth in them " ? (Ps. cxv. 3-11).

Or, substituting "bread" for wood and ashes, is there not a striking parallel to that graphic and vivid exposure, by the inspired prophet, of the blindness and folly of the idolater, of whom he says, "He feedeth on ashes: a deceived heart hath turned him aside, that he cannot deliver his soul, nor say, Is there not a lie in my right hand"?* (Isa. xliv. 30).

* See that parallel worked out in a striking manner by the Rev. Edward Nangle, in his book entitled, "*The Gospel Lever to overturn Romanism,*" published by the Religious Tract Society.

"Not unto us, O Lord, not unto us, but unto Thy name give glory, for Thy mercy, and for Thy truth's sake" (Ps. cxv. 1).

"Let not the wise man glory in his wisdom, neither let the mighty man glory in his might, let not the rich man glory in his riches. But let him that glorieth, glory in this, that he understandeth and knoweth Me, that I am the Lord, which exercise lovingkindness, judgment, and righteousness, in the earth : for in these things I delight, saith the Lord" (Jer. ix. 23, 24).

"For of Him, and through Him, and to Him, are all things : to whom be glory for ever. Amen" (Rom. xi. 36).

"Unto Him that loved us, and washed us from our sins in His own blood, and hath made us kings and priests unto God and His Father ; to Him be glory and dominion for ever and ever. Amen" (Rev. i. 5-7).

"And I heard as it were the voice of a great multitude, and as the voice of many waters, and as the voice of mighty thunderings, saying, "Alleluia : for the Lord God omnipotent reigneth" (Rev. xix. 1-9).

O

APPENDIX.

Since this Introduction was printed, a remarkable article on the Judgment has appeared in *The Times* of November 25th. After paying a high tribute to the character, erudition, and spirit evinced by the Archbishop personally, and to the "profound and laborious learning," as well as to the tone of the Judgment, the article proceeds to make some very weighty and suggestive remarks. Amongst them are the following :—

" The church has before it a judgment which, in addition to its official authority, will justly exert a great moral influence, and produce, in one way or another, a momentous effect. It may prove one of the turning points in the modern history of the English Church, and it will at least henceforth be one of the principal matters to be dealt with in the vital and enduring controversy by which it has been occasioned.

" But it is necessary to imitate the Archbishop himself in not allowing our respect for a great judgment to debar us from independent consideration of the circumstances with which it deals, and of its bearing upon them. He commences by saying that 'the Court has considered, with the utmost carefulness and respect, the various decisions which have been given in recent years upon some of the points at issue,' *but in the sequel the judgment proceeds on its own course, without attempting to come to an explanation or understanding with them.* New light, it is observed, has been thrown upon the subjects in question, and previous decisions of the Privy Council are accordingly disregarded when they are adverse to the independent conclusions of the Court. It will be for lawyers to judge how far this procedure is legitimate or effectual; but it will at least justify the application of the ordinary methods of public criticism to the judgment itself. Every one will bow with the utmost deference to the unanimous judgment of the Archbishop and his Assessors on the topics which they pass in review; but people will exercise their right to take account of other considerations of which the judgment takes little notice. Broadly speaking, the judgment authorizes the characteristic practices of the Bishop of Lincoln and his friends, but declares most positively and learnedly that they have no meaning or import whatever. The eastward position is declared to be legal throughout the Communion Service, but it has nothing whatever to do with the sacrificial aspect of the ordinance. Great and authoritative divines have said that it had, but they were mistaken; and no argument either for or against the practice can possibly be with fairness based on any doctrinal significance attached to it.

*　　*　　*　　*　　*

"So with the lights on the Holy Table. *In tacit reversal of the judgment of the Privy Council, they are adjudged not illegal,* but the increase in their use is treated as having merely gone along with an increased use of decoration, and it would be contrary to the history and interpretation of the two lights to connect them with erroneous and strange teaching as to the nature of the Sacrament. In short, the Ritualists are to have their way in the chief practices impugned.

*　　*　　*　　*　　*

"No significance," says the Archbishop, "can be attached to a form, act, or usage, unless that significance is in accordance with the regular and established meaning of language or symbol, whether liturgical or other." It is the only sentence in the Archbishop's judgment which seems to us at variance, unfortunately, with the evidence of historical fact.

*　　*　　*,　　*　　*

" Whatever the Ritualistic practices ought, or ought not, to mean, *no plain man can doubt that they have the practical effect of assimilating the administration of the Holy Communion to the celebration of the Mass, and that they are, at the very least, intended as a repudiation of Protestant doctrine on the subject. Men of great ability and piety—for it is their virtues which render them formidable—avowedly desire to upset the work of the Reformation in some important respects, and the very term of ' Protestant,' which was the pride of the highest of the*

High Church Divines of the Old School, such as Cosin, is repudiated by them. The opposite school—less strong, perhaps, at present among the clergy than among the laity—is not less earnestly opposed to this tendency, and it includes resolute men who may be expected to maintain their opposition to the last extremity.

" These being the plain and actual facts of the case, it is difficult to look forward without anxiety to the sequel of this memorable judgment. Peace is the greatest of blessings in the Church, and it is lamentable, as the Archbishop says, that attention should be diverted ' from the Church's real contest with evil and building ' up of good both by those who give and those who take offence unadvisedly,' in ' minute questionings and disputations in great and sacred subjects.' *But either the history of this country is a great illusion, or there is a real and vital issue at stake between Roman and Protestant principles, and common sense must allow that a great point is won according as the most solemn and characteristic ceremonies of the Church are made practically to speak one language or the other.* The difficulty unhappily in this case is not met by that toleration of diverse constructions which has gone far to solve some of the doctrinal controversies of the Church in the interpretation of the Articles. The thoughts of every member of a congregation are free in respect to the teaching of his clergyman; but if he goes to church at all, he is compelled to participate in the forms of worship adopted. If, indeed, he lives in a great town, he will probably have a choice of Churches within reach, and will find among them one or other at which he can worship with satisfaction. But in the country *the liberty of the clergyman is the bondage of the congregation. Any country village may suddenly have a priest imposed upon it who will transform its familiar and simple form of worship into an approximation to that of Rome, and every parishioner must either submit to it or give up his Church altogether.*"

The article concludes with these significant words : "But it requires a sanguine temperament to hope that either party will rise to the level either of the Archbishop's learning or of his moderation. If, however, the matter goes further, there arises the possibility of the highest lay Court overriding the highest spiritual Court; and what would then be the result?"

How far those extracts sustain much of the warp and woof of this book must be left to the judgment of the reader, particularly as regards the passages italicised by the writer.

The London papers have published an article headed, "The English Church Union and the Bishop of Lincoln." It begins thus :—

"Lord Halifax, the President of the English Church Union, has addressed to all the district unions and local branches, a letter on the subject of the Archbishop of Canterbury's judgment in the Bishop of Lincoln's case."

It closes with the following words :—

"The Archbishop's decision, setting on one side all

questions as to the canonical methods by which provincial jurisdiction should be exercised, affects the Bishop of Lincoln only, *but the principles and tenour of the judgment, vindicating as they do the historical rights and continuity of the Church of England*, are such as may well elicit, when they recall the history of the past, the thanks and gratitude of all loyal members of the Church of England."

From His Lordship's very pronounced opinions and sympathies in favour of the Church of Rome, no wonder that he rejoices at "the principles and tenour of the judgment," which, as the *Times* points out, is in favour of the Ritualists, and opposed to the principles of the Reformation, and to the teaching of the Church of England *at the present time*. Logically and consistently, then, "*the historical rights and continuity of the Church of England*" vindicated by the judgment, and endorsed by Lord Halifax and the English Church Union, must be those enjoyed by her before the *Reformation from Popery*. If so, how can that party be consistently "loyal members of the [*Reformed*] Church of England?"

Henderson & Spalding, Printers, 3 & 5, Marylebone Lane, W.